Praise for Kyung-sook Shin's
Please Look After Mom

"The most moving and accomplished, and often startling, novel in translation I've read in many seasons. . . . Every sentence is saturated in detail. . . . It tells an almost unbearably affecting story of remorse and belated wisdom that reminds us how globalism—at the human level—can tear souls apart and leave them uncertain of where to turn."
—Pico Iyer, *The Wall Street Journal*

"The novel perfectly combines universal themes of love and loss, family dynamics, gender equality, tradition, and charity with the rich Korean culture and values which make *Please Look After Mom* a great literary masterpiece."
—*Seattle Post-Intelligencer*

"An authentic, moving story that brings to vivid life the deep family connections that lie at the core of Korean culture. But it also speaks beautifully to an urgent issue of our time: migration, and how the movement of people from small towns and villages to big cities can cause heartbreak and even tragedy. This is a tapestry of family life that will be read all over the world. I loved this book." —Gary Shteyngart,
author of *Super Sad True Love Story*

"Haunting. . . . The novel's language—so formal in its simplicity—bestows a grace and solemnity on childhood scenes that might otherwise be overwrought. . . . Throughout the novel, the rhythms of agrarian life and labor that Shin deftly conveys have a subtle, cumulative power."

—*The Boston Globe*

"Well-controlled and emotionally taut. . . . What distinguishes this novel is the way it questions whether our pasts, either public or private, are really available for us to recollect and treasure anyway."

—*Financial Times*

"A captivating story, written with an understanding of the shortcomings of traditional ways of modern life. It is nostalgic but unsentimental, brutally well observed and, in this flawlessly smooth translation by Chi-Young Kim, it offers a sobering account of a vanished past. . . . We must hope there will be more translations to follow."

—*Times Literary Supplement*

"A poignant story of a family told in four voices. . . . Shin's storytelling and her gift for detail make *Please Look After Mom* a book worth reading."

—*Post and Courier*

"Here is a deeply felt journey into a culture foreign to many—yet with a theme that is universal in its appeal. A terrific novel that stayed with me long after I'd finished its final, haunting pages. This is a real discovery."

—Abraham Verghese,
author of *Cutting for Stone*

"Here is a wonderful, original new voice, by turns plangent and piquant. *Please Look After Mom* takes us on a dual journey, to the unfamiliar corners of a foreign culture and into the shadowy recesses of the heart. In spare, exquisite prose, Kyung-sook Shin penetrates the very essence of what it means to be a family, and a human being." —Geraldine Brooks, Pulitzer Prize–winning author of *March*

"Shin is a scribe with a slow and steady pulse; this is writing that allows you to meander with your own thoughts (and reflect on your own mother, perhaps), while still following the physical and mental travels of her characters. . . . Plain and softy insistent eloquence." —*Hyphen Magazine*

"Intriguing. . . . It is easy to see the source of this global popularity, for not only is Shin's absorbing novel written with considerable grace and suspense, but she also has managed to tap into a universality: the inequitable relationship between a mother and her children." —*BookPage*

"An arresting account of the misunderstandings that can cloud the beauty of the affection and memories that bind two very different generations. . . . A touching story that effectively weaves the rural, ages-old lifestyle of a mother into the modern urban lives of her children." —*The Star-Ledger* (Newark)

Kyung-sook Shin

Please Look After Mom

Kyung-sook Shin is the author of numerous works of fiction and is one of South Korea's most widely read and acclaimed novelists. She has been honored with the Manhae Literature Prize, the Dong-in Literature Prize, and the Yi Sang Literary Prize, as well as France's Prix de l'Inaperçu. *Please Look After Mom* is her first book to appear in English. It will be published in twenty-three countries and has sold almost 1.5 million copies in South Korea alone.

Please Look After Mom

Please Look After Mom

A NOVEL

Kyung-sook Shin

TRANSLATED FROM THE KOREAN
BY CHI-YOUNG KIM

Vintage Canada

Published in Canada by Vintage Canada, a division of Random House of Canada
Limited, Toronto, in 2012, and simultaneously in the United States of America
by Vintage Books, a division of Random House Inc., New York. Originally published in hardcover in Canada by Random House Canada, a division of Random
House of Canada Limited, in 2011, and simultaneously in the United States of
America by Alfred A. Knopf, a division of Random House Inc., New York. Distributed in Canada by Random House of Canada Limited.

Originally published in slightly different form in South Korea as *Ŏmma rŭl
Put'akhae* by Changbi Publishers, P'aju-si Kyŏnggi-do, in 2008. Copyright © 2008
by Kyung-sook Shin.

Vintage Canada with colophon is a registered trademark.

www.randomhouse.ca

Library and Archives Canada Cataloguing in Publication

Shin, Kyung-sook
Please look after mom / Kyung-sook Shin ; translated by Chi-Young Kim.

Translation of: Eommareul Butakhae.
Issued also in electronic format.

ISBN 978-0-307-35920-9

I. Kim, Chi-Young II. Title.

PL992.73.K94O4613 2012   895.7'34   C2010-904934-9

Book design by Soonyoung Kwon
Image credits: marc fischer/Getty Images
Printed and bound in the United States of America

2 4 6 8 9 7 5 3 1

O love, so long as you can love.

—FRANZ LISZT

Contents

Nobody Knows

IT'S BEEN ONE WEEK since Mom went missing.

The family is gathered at your eldest brother Hyong-chol's house, bouncing ideas off each other. You decide to make flyers and hand them out where Mom was last seen. The first thing to do, everyone agrees, is to draft a flyer. Of course, a flyer is an old-fashioned response to a crisis like this. But there are few things a missing person's family can do, and the missing person is none other than your mom. All you can do is file a missing-person report, search the area, ask passersby if they have seen anyone who looks like her. Your younger brother, who owns an online clothing store, says he posted something about your mother's disappearance, describing where she went missing; he uploaded her picture and asked people to contact the family if they'd seen her. You want to go look for her in places where you think she might be, but you know how she is: she can't go anywhere by herself in this city. Hyong-chol designates you to write up the flyer, since you write for a living. You blush, as if you were caught doing something you shouldn't. You aren't sure how helpful your words will be in finding Mom.

When you write July 24, 1938, as Mom's birth date, your father corrects you, saying that she was born in 1936. Official records show that she was born in 1938, but apparently she was born in 1936. This is the first time you've heard this. Your father says everyone did that, back in the day. Because many children didn't survive their first three months, people raised them for a few years before making it official. When you're about to rewrite "38" as "36," Hyong-chol says you have to write 1938, because that's the official date. You don't think you need to be so precise when you're only making homemade flyers and it isn't like you're at a government office. But you obediently leave "38," wondering if July 24 is even Mom's real birthday.

A few years ago, your mom said, "We don't have to celebrate my birthday separately." Father's birthday is one month before Mom's. You and your siblings always went to your parents' house in Chongup for birthdays and other celebrations. All together, there were twenty-two people in the immediate family. Mom liked it when all of her children and grandchildren gathered and bustled about the house. A few days before everyone came down, she would make fresh kimchi, go to the market to buy beef, and stock up on extra toothpaste and toothbrushes. She pressed sesame oil and roasted and ground sesame and perilla seeds, so she could present her children with a jar of each as they left. As she waited for the family to arrive, your mom would be visibly animated, her words and her gestures revealing her pride when she talked to neighbors or acquaintances. In the shed, Mom kept glass bottles of every size filled with plum or wild-strawberry juice, which she made seasonally. Mom's jars were filled to the brim with tiny fermented croakerlike fish or anchovy paste or fermented clams that she was planning to send to the family in the city. When she heard that onions were good for one's health, she made onion juice, and before winter came, she made pumpkin juice infused with licorice. Your mom's house was like a factory; she prepared sauces and fermented bean paste and hulled rice, producing things for the family year-round. At some point, the children's trips to Chongup became less frequent, and Mom and Father started to come to Seoul more often. And then you began to celebrate each of their birthdays by going out for dinner. That was easier. Then Mom even suggested, "Let's celebrate my birthday on your father's." She said it would be a burden to celebrate their birthdays separately, since both happen during the hot summer, when there are also two ancestral rites only two days apart. At first the family refused to do that, even when Mom insisted on it, and if she balked at coming to the city, a few of you went home to celebrate with her. Then you all started to give Mom her birthday gift on Father's birthday. Eventually, quietly, Mom's actual birthday was bypassed.

Mom, who liked to buy socks for everyone in the family, had in her dresser a growing collection of socks that her children didn't take.

NAME: Park So-nyo

DATE OF BIRTH: July 24, 1938 (69 years old)

APPEARANCE: Short, salt-and-pepper permed hair, prominent cheekbones, last seen wearing a sky-blue shirt, a white jacket, and a beige pleated skirt.

LAST SEEN: Seoul Station subway

Nobody can decide which picture of Mom you should use. Everyone agrees it should be the most recent picture, but nobody has a recent picture of her. You remember that at some point Mom started to hate getting her picture taken. She would sneak away even for family portraits. The most recent photograph of Mom is a family picture taken at Father's seventieth-birthday party. Mom looked nice in a pale-blue hanbok, with her hair done at a salon, and she was even wearing red lipstick. Your younger brother thinks your mom looks so different in this picture from the way she did right before she went missing. He doesn't think people would identify her as the same person, even if her image is isolated and enlarged. He reports that when he posted this picture of her, people responded by saying, "Your mother is pretty, and she doesn't seem like the kind of person who would get lost." You all decide to see if anyone has another picture of Mom. Hyong-chol tells you to write something more on the flyer. When you stare at him, he tells you to think of better sentences, to tug on the reader's heartstrings. Words that would tug on the reader's heartstrings? When you write, *Please help us find our mother,* he says it's too plain. When you write, *Our mother is missing,* he says that "mother" is too formal, and tells you to write "mom." When you write, *Our mom is missing,* he decides it's too childish. When you write, *Please contact us if you see this person,* he barks, "What kind of writer are you?" You can't think of a single sentence that would satisfy Hyong-chol.

Your second-eldest brother says, "You'd tug on people's heartstrings if you write that there will be a reward."

When you write, *We will reward you generously,* your sister-in-law says you can't write like that: people take notice only if you write a specific amount.

"So how much should I say?"

"One million won?"

"That's not enough."

"Three million won?"

"I think that's too little, too."

"Then five million won."

Nobody complains about five million won. You write, *We will reward you with five million won,* and put in a period. Your second-eldest brother says you should write it as, *Reward: 5 million won.* Your younger brother tells you to put *5 million won* in a bigger font. Everyone agrees to e-mail you a better picture of Mom if they find something. You're in charge of adding more to the flyer and making copies, and your younger brother volunteers to pick them up and distribute them to everyone in the family. When you suggest, "We can hire someone to give out flyers," Hyong-chol says, "We're the ones who need to do that. We'll give them out on our own if we have some free time during the week, and all together over the weekend."

You grumble, "How will we ever find Mom at that rate?"

"We can't just sit tight; we're already doing everything we can," Hyong-chol retorts.

"What do you mean, we're doing everything we can?"

"We put ads in the newspaper."

"So doing everything we can is buying ad space?"

"Then what do you want to do? Should we all quit work tomorrow and just roam around the city? If we could find Mom like that, I'd do it."

You stop arguing with Hyong-chol, because you realize that you're pushing him to take care of everything, as you always do. Leaving Father at Hyong-chol's house, you all head home. If you don't leave then, you will continue to argue. You've been doing that for the past week. You'd meet to discuss how to find Mom, and one of you would unexpectedly dig up the different ways someone else had wronged her in the past. The things that had been suppressed, that had been carefully avoided moment by moment, became bloated, and finally you all yelled and smoked and banged out the door in a rage.

When you first heard Mom had gone missing, you angrily asked why nobody from your large family went to pick her and Father up at Seoul Station.

"And where were you?"

Me? You clammed up. You didn't find out about Mom's disappearance until she'd been gone four days. You all blamed each other for Mom's going missing, and you all felt wounded.

Leaving Hyong-chol's house, you take the subway home but get off at Seoul Station, which is where Mom vanished. So many people go by, brushing your shoulders, as you make your way to the spot where Mom was last seen. You look down at your watch. Three o'clock. The same time Mom was left behind. People shove past you as you stand on the platform where Mom was wrenched from Father's grasp. Not a single person apologizes to you. People would have pushed by like that as your mom stood there, not knowing what to do.

How far back does one's memory of someone go? Your memory of Mom?

Since you heard about Mom's disappearance, you haven't been able to focus on a single thought, besieged by long-forgotten memories unexpectedly popping up. And the regret that always trailed each memory. Years ago, a few days before you left your hometown for the big city, Mom took you to a clothing store at the market. You chose a plain dress, but she picked one with frills on the straps and hem. "What about this one?"

"No," you said, pushing it away.

"Why not? Try it on." Mom, young back then, opened her eyes wide, uncomprehending. The frilly dress was worlds away from the dirty towel that was always wrapped around Mom's head, which, like other farming women, she wore to soak up the sweat on her brow as she worked.

"It's childish."

"Is it?" Mom said, but she held the dress up and kept

examining it, as if she didn't want to walk away. "I would try it on if I were you."

Feeling bad that you'd called it childish, you said, "This isn't even your style."

Mom said, "No, I like these kinds of clothes, it's just that I've never been able to wear them."

I should have tried on that dress. You bend your legs and squat on the spot where Mom might have done the same. A few days after you insisted on buying the plain dress, you arrived at this very station with Mom. Holding your hand tightly, she strode through the sea of people in a way that would intimidate even the authoritative buildings looking on from above, and headed across the square to wait for Hyong-chol under the clock tower. How could someone like that be missing? As the headlights of the subway train enter the station, people rush forward, glancing at you sitting on the ground, perhaps irritated that you're in the way.

As your mom's hand got pulled away from Father's, you were in China. You were with your fellow writers at the Beijing Book Fair. You were flipping through a Chinese translation of your book at a booth when your mom got lost in Seoul Station.

"Father, why didn't you take a cab instead? This wouldn't have happened if you hadn't taken the subway!"

Father said he was thinking, Why take a taxi when the train station is connected to the subway station? There are moments one revisits after something happens, especially after something bad happens. Moments in which one thinks, I shouldn't have done that. When Father told your siblings that he and Mom could get to Hyong-chol's house by themselves, why did your siblings let them do that, unlike all the other times? When your parents came to visit, someone always went to Seoul Station or to the Express Bus Terminal to pick them up. What made Father, who always rode in a family member's car or a taxi when he came to the city, decide to take the subway on that particular day? Mom and Father rushed toward the subway that had just arrived. Father got on, and when he looked behind him, Mom wasn't there. Of all days, it was a busy Saturday afternoon. Mom was pulled away from Father in the crowd, and the subway left as she tried to get her bearings. Father was holding Mom's bag. So, when Mom was left alone in the subway station with nothing, you were leaving the book fair, headed toward Tiananmen Square. It was your third time in Beijing, but you hadn't yet set foot in Tiananmen Square, had only gazed at it from inside a bus or a car. The student who was guiding your group offered to take you there before going to dinner, and your group decided it was a good idea. What would your mom have been doing by herself in Seoul Station as you got out of the cab in front of the Forbidden City? Your group walked into the Forbidden City but came right back out. That landmark was only partially open, because it was under construction, and it was almost closing time. The entire city of Beijing was under construction, to prepare for the Olympic Games the following year. You remembered the scene in *The Last Emperor* where the elderly Puyi returns to the Forbidden City, his childhood home, and shows a young tourist a box he had hidden in the throne. When he opens the lid of the box, his pet cricket from his youth is inside, still alive. When you were about to head over to Tiananmen Square, was your mom standing in the middle of the crowd, lost, being jostled? Was she waiting for someone to come get her? The road between the Forbidden City and Tiananmen Square was under construction, too. You could see the square, but you could get there only through a convoluted maze. As you watched the kites floating in the sky in Tiananmen Square, your mom might have collapsed in the passageway in despair, calling out your name. As you watched the steel gates of Tiananmen Square open and a squadron of police march forth, legs raised high, to lower the red national flag with five stars, your mom might have been wandering through the maze inside Seoul Station. You know this to be true, because that's what the people who were in the station at that time told you. They said they saw an old woman walking very slowly, sometimes sitting on the floor or standing vacantly by the escalators. Some saw an old woman sitting in the station for a long time, then getting on an arriving subway. A few hours after your mom disappeared, you and your group took a taxi through the nighttime city to bright, bustling Snack Street and, huddled under red lights, tasted 56-proof Chinese liquor and ate piping-hot crab sautéed in chili oil.

Father got off at the next stop and went back to Seoul Station, but Mom wasn't there anymore.

"How could she get so lost just because she didn't get on the same car? There are signs all over the place. Mother knows how to make a simple phone call. She could have called from a phone booth." Your sister-in-law insisted that something had to have happened to your mom, that it didn't make sense that she couldn't find her own son's house just because she failed to get on the same train as Father. Something had happened to Mom. That was the view of someone who wanted to think of Mom as the old mom.

When you said, "Mom can get lost, you know," your sister-in-law widened her eyes in surprise. "You know how Mom is these days," you explained, and your sister-in-law made a face, as if she had no idea what you were talking about. But your family knew what Mom was like these days. And knew that you might not be able to find her.

———

When was it you realized that Mom didn't know how to read?

You wrote your first letter when you jotted down what Mom dictated to send to Hyong-chol, soon after he moved to the city. Hyong-chol graduated from high school in the small village you were all born in, studied at home for the civil-service exam for a year, and went to the city for his first assignment. It was the first parting between Mom and one of her children. Back then, your family didn't have a phone, and the only way to communicate was through letters. Hyong-chol sent her letters written in large type. Your mom always intuitively knew when Hyong-chol's letters would arrive. The mailman came around eleven in the morning with a large bag hanging from his bicycle. On the days when Hyong-chol's letters arrived, Mom would come in from the fields, or from the creek where she would be doing the laundry, to receive the letter personally from the mailman. Then she waited for you to come home from school, led you to the back porch, and took out Hyong-chol's letter. "Read it out loud," she would tell you.

Hyong-chol's letters always started with "Dearest Mother." As if he were following a textbook on how to write letters, Hyong-chol asked after the family and said he was doing well. He wrote that he brought his laundry to Father's cousin's wife once a week, and that she washed it for him, as Mom had asked her to do. He reported that he was eating well, that he had found a place to sleep as he had started staying overnight at work, and asked her not to worry about him. Hyong-chol also wrote that he felt he could do anything in the city, and that there were many things he wanted to do. He even revealed his ambition to become a success and give Mom a better life. Twenty-year-old Hyong-chol gallantly added, *So, Mother, do not worry about me, and please take care of your health.* When you peeked over the letter at Mom, you would see her staring at the taro stalks in the back yard, or at the ledge of tall clay jars filled with sauces. Your mom's ears would be cocked like a rabbit's, trying not to miss a single word. After you finished reading the letter, your mom instructed you to write down what she would tell you. Mom's first words were "Dear Hyong-chol." You wrote down, *Dear Hyong-chol*. Mom didn't tell you to put a period after it, but you did. When she said, "Hyong-chol!" you wrote down, *Hyong-chol!* When Mom paused after calling his name, as if she'd forgotten what she wanted to say, you tucked strands of your bob behind your ear and waited attentively for your mom to continue, ballpoint pen in hand, staring down at the stationery. When she said, "The weather's turned cold," you wrote, *The weather has turned cold.* Mom always followed "Dear Hyong-chol" with something about the weather: "There are flowers now that it's spring." "It's summer, so the paddy bed is starting to dry and crack." "It's harvest season, and there are beans overflowing on the paddy banks." Mom spoke in your regional dialect unless it was to dictate a letter to Hyong-chol. "Don't worry about anything at home, and please take care of yourself. That is the only thing your mother wishes from you." Mom's letters always swelled with a current of emotion: "I am sorry that I can't be of any help to you." As you carefully wrote down Mom's words, she would shed a fat tear. The last words from your mom were always the same: "Make sure you eat all your meals. Mom."

As the third of five children, you witnessed Mom's sorrow and pain and worry when each of your older brothers left home. Every morning at dawn after Hyong-chol left, Mom would clean the surface of the glazed clay sauce-jars on the ledge in the back yard. Because the well was in the front yard, it was cumbersome to bring water to the back, but she washed each and every jar. She took off all the lids and wiped them clean, inside and out, until they shone. Your mom sang quietly. "If there were no sea between you and me there wouldn't be this painful goodbye. . . ." Her hands busily dipping the rag in cold water and lifting it out and wringing it and rubbing the jars, Mom sang, "I hope you won't leave me one day." If you called to her at that moment, she would turn around with tears welling in her big, guileless eyes.

Mom's love for Hyong-chol was such that she used to make a bowl of ramen only for him, when he came home after remaining at school till late at night to study. Later, when you brought that up sometimes, your boyfriend, Yu-bin, would reply, "It's just ramen—what's the big deal?"

"What do you mean, what's the big deal? Ramen was the best thing back then! It was something you ate in secret so you wouldn't have to share it!" Even though you explained its significance, he, a city boy, seemed to think it was nothing.

When this new delicacy called ramen entered your lives, it overwhelmed every dish Mom had ever made. Mom would buy ramen and hide it in an empty jar in the row of clay jars, wanting to save it for Hyong-chol. But even late at night, the smell of boiling ramen would nudge you and your siblings awake. When Mom said, sternly, "You all go back to bed," you would all look at Hyong-chol, who was about to eat. Feeling sorry, he would offer each of you a bite. Mom would remark, "How is it that you all come so quickly when it has to do with food?" and fill the pot with water, make another ramen, and divide it among you and your siblings. You would be so pleased, each holding a bowl filled with more soup than noodles.

After Hyong-chol had left for the city, when Mom reached the clay jar she used to hide the ramen in, she would call out, "Hyong-chol!" and sink down, her legs giving way. You would slip the rag from Mom's grasp, lift her arm up, and drape it around your shoulder. Your mom would break out in sobs, unable to control her overflowing feelings for her firstborn.

When Mom sank into sorrow after your brothers left, the only things you could do for her were to read your brothers' letters out loud, and to slip her responses into the mailbox on the way to school. Even then, you had no idea that she had never once set foot in the world of letters. Why did it never occur to you that Mom didn't know how to read or write, even when she relied on you as a child, even after you read her the letters and wrote replies for her? You took her request as just another chore, similar to heading out to the garden to pick some mallow or going to buy some kerosene. Mom must not have given that task to anyone else after you left home, because you never received a letter from her. Was it because you didn't write her? It was probably because of the phone. Around the time you left for the city, a public phone was installed in the village head's house. It was the first phone in your birthplace, a small farming community where, once in a while, a train would clatter along tracks that stretched between the village and the vast fields. Every morning, the villagers heard the village head testing the mike then announcing that so and so should come over to answer a call from Seoul. Your brothers started to call the public phone. After the phone was installed, people who had family in other cities paid attention to the sounds of the microphone, even from paddies or fields, wondering who was being sought.

———

Either a mother and daughter know each other very well, or they are strangers.

Until last fall, you thought you knew your mom well—what Mom liked, what you had to do to appease her when she was angry, what she wanted to hear. If someone asked you what Mom was doing, you could answer in ten seconds: she's probably drying ferns; since it's Sunday, she must be at church. But last fall, your belief that you knew her was shattered. You went for a visit without announcing it beforehand, and you discovered that you had become a guest. Mom was continually embarrassed about the messy yard or the dirty blankets. At one point, she grabbed a towel from the floor and hung it, and when food dropped on the table, she picked it up quickly. She took a look at what she had in the fridge, and even though you tried to stop her, she went to the market. If you are with family, you needn't feel embarrassed about leaving the table uncleared after a meal and going to do something else. You realized you'd become a stranger as you watched Mom try to conceal her messy everyday life.

Maybe you'd become a guest even before then, when you moved to the city. After you left home, your mom never scolded you. Before, Mom would reprimand you harshly if you did something even remotely wrong. From when you were young, Mom always addressed you as "You, girl." Usually she said that to you and your sister when she wanted to differentiate between her daughters and sons, but your mom also called you "You, girl" when she demanded that you correct your habits, disapproving of your way of eating fruit, your walk, your clothes, and your style of speech. But sometimes she would become worried and look closely into your face. She studied you with a concerned expression when she needed your help to pull flat the corners of starched blanket covers, or when she had you put kindling in the old-fashioned kitchen furnace to cook rice. One cold winter day, you and your mom were at the well, cleaning the skate that would be used for the ancestral rites at New Year's, when she said, "You have to work hard in school so that you can move into a better world." Did you understand her words then? When Mom scolded you freely, you more frequently called her Mom. The word "Mom" is familiar and it hides a plea: *Please look after me. Please stop yelling at me and stroke my head; please be on my side, whether I'm right or wrong.* You never stopped calling her Mom. Even now, when Mom's missing. When you call out "Mom," you want to believe that she's healthy. That Mom is strong. That Mom isn't fazed by anything. That Mom is the person you want to call whenever you despair about something in this city.

Last fall, you didn't tell her that you were coming down, but it wasn't to free your mom from preparing for your arrival. You were in Pohang at the time. Your parents' house was far from Pohang, where you arrived on an early-morning flight. Even when you got up at dawn and washed your hair and left for the airport, you didn't know that you were going to go see Mom in Chongup. It was farther and more difficult to go to Chongup from Pohang than from Seoul. It wasn't something you'd expected to do.

. . .

When you got to your parents' house, the gate was open. The front door was open, too. You had a lunch date with Yubin back in the city the next day, so you were going to return home on the night train. Even though you were born there, the village had become an unfamiliar place. The only things left from your childhood were the three nettle trees, now mature, near the creek. When you went to your parents' house, you took the small path toward the nettle-lined creek instead of the big road. If you kept going that way, it would lead you straight to the back gate of your childhood home. A long time ago, there was a communal well right outside the back gate. The well was filled in when modern plumbing was installed in every house, but you stood on that spot before entering the house. You tapped the sturdy cement with your foot, precisely where that abundant well used to be. You were overwhelmed with nostalgia. What would the well be doing in the darkness under the street, the well that had supplied water to all the people in the alley and still sloshed about? You weren't there when the well was filled in. One day you went back for a visit and the well was gone, just a cement road where it had been. Probably because you didn't see the well being filled with your own eyes, you couldn't stop imagining that the well was still there, brimming with water, under the cement.

You stood above the well for a while, then went through the gate, calling, "Mom!" But she didn't answer. The setting autumn sunlight filled the yard of the house, which faced west. You went into the house to look for her, but she wasn't in the living room or in the bedroom. The house was a mess. A water bottle stood open on the table, and a cup was perched on the edge of the sink. A basket of rags was overturned on the floor mat in the living room, and hanging on the sofa was a dirty shirt with its sleeves flung apart, as if Father had just taken it off. The late-afternoon sun was illuminating the empty space. "Mom!" Even though you knew nobody was there, you called one more time, "Mom!" You walked out the front door and, in the side yard, discovered Mom lying on the wooden platform in the doorless shed. "Mom!" you called, but there was no reply. You put on your shoes and walked toward the shed. From there you could look over the yard. A long time ago, Mom had brewed malt in the shed. It was a useful space, especially after it was expanded into the adjacent pigsty. She piled old, unused kitchen supplies on the shelves she had mounted on a wall, and underneath there were glass jars of things she had pickled and preserved. It was Mom who had moved the wooden platform into the shed. After the old house was torn down and a Western-style house was built, she would sit on the platform to do kitchen work that she couldn't easily do in the modern kitchen inside. She would grind red peppers in the mortar to make kimchi, sift through beanstalks to find beans and shuck them, make red-pepper paste, salt cabbage for winter kimchi, or dry fermented soybean cakes.

The doghouse next to the shed was vacant, the dog chain lying on the ground. You realized that you hadn't heard the dog when you walked into the house. Looking around for him, you approached Mom, but she didn't move. She must have been cutting zucchini to dry in the sun. A chopping board, a knife, and zucchini were pushed to the side, and small slices of zucchini were cradled in a worn bamboo basket. At first you wondered, Is Mom sleeping? Recalling that she wasn't one to take naps, you peered into her face. Mom had a hand clutching her head, and she was struggling with all her might. Her lips were parted, and she was frowning so intently that her face was gnarled with deep wrinkles.

"Mom!"

She didn't open her eyes.

"Mom! Mom!"

You knelt in front of Mom and shook her hard, and her eyes opened slightly. They were bloodshot, and beads of sweat dotted her forehead. Your mom didn't seem to recognize you. Weighted with pain, her face was a miserable knot. Only some invisible malevolence could cause an expression like that. She closed her eyes again.

"Mom!"

You scrambled onto the platform and cradled your mom's tortured face on your lap. You hooked your arm under her armpit, so that her head wouldn't slide off your knees. How could she be left alone in this state? Outrage flashed through your conscience, as if someone had tossed her in the shed like that. But you were the one who had moved away and left your mom's side. If one is deeply shocked, one cannot figure out what to do. *Should I call an ambulance? Should I move her into the house? Where's Father?* These thoughts raced through your head, but you ended up gazing down at Mom lying across your lap. You had never seen her face contorted like that, so miserable, in such pain. Her hand, which was pressing down on her forehead, fell listlessly to the platform. Mom breathed laboriously, exhausted. Her limbs drooped, as if she could no longer exert the effort to try to avoid the pain. "Mom!" Your heart pounded. It occurred to you that she might be dying, just like this. But then Mom's eyes opened calmly and trained themselves on you. It should have surprised her to see you, but there was nothing in her eyes. She appeared to be too weak to react. A while later, she called your name, her face dull. And she mumbled something faintly. You leaned in.

"When my sister died I couldn't even cry." Mom's pale face was so hollow that you couldn't say a thing.

Your aunt's funeral was in the spring. You didn't go. You hadn't even visited her, although she had been sick for almost a year. And what were you doing instead? When you were young, your aunt was your second mom. During summer vacations you went to live with her, in her house just on the other side of the mountain. Your aunt had the closest relationship with you among all of your siblings. It was probably because you looked like Mom. Your aunt always said, "You and your mother are cast from the same mold!" As if she were re-creating her childhood with her sister, your aunt fed rabbits with you and braided your hair. She cooked a pot of barley with a scoop of rice on top and saved the rice for you. At night you lay across her lap and listened to the stories she told you. You remembered how your aunt used to slide an arm under your neck at night to fashion a pillow for you. Even though she had left this world, you still remembered your aunt's scent from those childhood visits. She spent her old age looking after her grandchildren, while their parents ran a bakery. Your aunt fell down the stairs as she was carrying a child on her back, and was rushed to the hospital, where she found out that cancer had spread through her body to such an extent that it was too late to do anything. Your mom told you the news. "My poor older sister!"

"Why didn't they catch it until now?"

"She'd never even gone in for a checkup."

Your mom visited her sister with porridge and spooned some into her mouth. You listened quietly when your mom called to say, "Yesterday I went to see your aunt. I made sesame porridge, and she had a good appetite." You were the first one Mom called when she found out that your aunt had died.

"My sister died."

You didn't say anything.

"You don't need to come, since you're busy."

Even if your mom hadn't said that, you wouldn't have been able to go to your aunt's funeral, because you had a deadline coming up. Hyong-chol, who went to the funeral, told you that he had been worried that Mom would be devastated, but she didn't cry, and she told him she didn't want to go to the burial grounds. "Really?" you'd asked. Hyong-chol said he thought it was strange, too, but he honored her wishes.

In the shed that day, Mom, whose face was marred with pain, told you she couldn't even cry when her sister died.

"Why not? You should have cried if you wanted to," you said, feeling a little relieved that she was returning to the Mom you knew, even though she spoke without revealing any emotion.

Your mom blinked placidly. "I can't cry anymore."

You didn't say anything.

"Because then my head hurts so much it feels like it's going to explode."

With the setting sun warming your back, you gazed down at Mom's face cradled on your lap as if it were the first time you were seeing it. Mom got headaches? So severe that she couldn't even cry? Her dark eyes, which used to be as brilliant and round as the eyes of a cow that is about to give birth, were hidden under wrinkles. Her pale, fat lips were dry and cracked. You picked up her arm, which she'd flung on the platform, and placed it on her stomach. You stared at the dark sunspots on the back of her hand, saturated with a lifetime of labor. You could no longer say you knew Mom.

———

When your uncle was alive, he would come to see Mom every Wednesday. He had just returned to Chongup, after a nomadic life of roaming the country. There was no specific reason for the visit; he just rode in on his bike and saw Mom and left. Sometimes, instead of coming into the house, he called from the gate, "Sister! Doing well?" Then, before your mom could get out to the yard, he called, "I'm going now!" and turned his bike around and left. As far as you knew, Mom and her brother were not that close. At some point before you were born, your uncle had borrowed quite a lot of money from Father, but he never paid it back. Your mom sometimes brought that up, bitterly. She said, because of your uncle, she always felt indebted to Father and Father's sister. Even though it was your uncle's debt, it was hard for your mom to come to terms with the knowledge that he didn't pay it back. When four or five years went by without news from your uncle, your mom always wondered, "What could your uncle be doing these days?" You couldn't tell if Mom was worrying about him or resenting him.

One day, your mom heard someone push the gate open and enter, saying, "Sister, are you in?" Mom, who was inside eating tangerines with you, threw open the door and ran out. It happened so quickly. Who was it that got her so excited? Curious, you followed her out. Mom paused on the porch, looking at the gate, shouted, "Brother!" to the person standing next to it, and ran to him—not caring that she was barefoot. It was your uncle. Your mom, who had run out like the wind, beat his chest with her fist and cried, "Brother! Brother!" You watched her from the porch. It was the first time you had heard her call someone "Brother." When she referred to her brother, she always called him "your uncle." You don't understand why you were so surprised when you saw Mom run to your uncle and call him "Brother" in a delighted nasal tone, when you had known all along that you had an uncle. You realized, Oh, Mom has a brother, too! Sometimes you laughed to yourself when you remembered what your mom was like that day, your aging mom jumping down from the porch and running across the yard to your uncle, shouting "Brother!" as if she were a child—Mom acting like a girl even younger than you. That mom was stuck in your head. It made you think, even Mom . . . You don't understand why it took you so long to realize something so obvious. To you, Mom was always Mom. It never occurred to you that she had once taken her first step, or had once been three or twelve or twenty years old. Mom was Mom. She was born as Mom. Until you saw her running to your uncle like that, it hadn't dawned on you that she was a human being who harbored the exact same feeling you had for your own brothers, and this realization led to the awareness that she, too, had had a childhood. From then on, you sometimes thought of Mom as a child, as a girl, as a young woman, as a newlywed, as a mother who had just given birth to you.

———

You couldn't leave Mom and return to the city after seeing her like that in the shed. Father was in Sokcho, with some people from the Regional Center for Korean Traditional Performing Arts. He was supposed to be home in two days. Although Mom got over the severe pain, she couldn't free herself from the headache, and she couldn't crack a smile, let alone cry. She couldn't even understand your suggestion that she should go to the hospital. When you helped her into the house, she walked gingerly, trying to keep her pain in check. A long time passed before she could talk. Mom said that she always got headaches but only had terrible ones "once in a while," and that she could put up with it since those moments passed.

Did your siblings know about Mom's headaches? Did Father?

You wanted to tell them, and to take her to a big hospital as soon as you returned to the city. When she was able to move around by herself, Mom asked, "Don't you need to go back?" At some point your visits home had become shorter; you would come for only a few hours and return to the city. You thought of your date the next day, but told your mom that you were going to stay the night. You remember the smile that spread across her face.

You left the live octopus you'd bought at the Pohang fish market in the kitchen, since neither you nor your mom knew what to do with it, and you sat across from Mom at the table like old times, quietly eating a simple meal of rice and panchan, side dishes of water kimchi, braised tofu, sautéed anchovies, and toasted seaweed. When Mom wrapped a piece of seaweed around some rice, as she did when you were little, and held it out, you took it and ate it. After dinner, to digest the food, you and Mom walked around the outside of the house. It was no longer the same house you grew up in, but the front, side, and back yards were still connected, like before. In the back yard, on the ledge, there were still so many tall clay jars. When you were young, they were filled with soy sauce, red-pepper paste, salt, and bean paste, but now they were empty. As the two of you walked, Mom sometimes leading and sometimes falling behind, she suddenly asked you why you'd come home.

"I went to Pohang. . . ."

"Pohang is far from here."

"Yeah."

"It's farther to come here from Pohang than from Seoul."

"Yeah, it is."

"What made you come here from Pohang, when it seems like you don't ever have time to visit?"

Instead of answering, you grabbed Mom's hand, desperately, as if you were grasping for a lifeline in the darkness, because you didn't know how to explain your emotions. You told Mom that in the early morning you had gone to lecture at a Braille library in Pohang.

"A Braille library?" Mom asked.

"Braille is what the blind read with their fingers."

Mom nodded. As you circled the house, you told Mom about your trip to Pohang. For a few years, the Braille library had been asking you to visit, but each time you couldn't because of a previous engagement. In early spring, you'd received another call. You had just published your latest work. The librarian told you that they wanted to publish your newest book in Braille. Braille! You didn't know much about it, except that it was the language of the blind, as you told Mom. You listened to the librarian impassively, as if you were hearing about a book you hadn't yet read. The librarian said they wanted your permission. If the librarian hadn't said "permission," you might not have agreed to go to the Braille library. That word "permission" moved you: blind people wanted to read your book, they were asking for your permission to recreate your book in a language only they could communicate through. . . . You answered, "Sure," suddenly feeling powerless. The librarian said that the book would be completed by

November, and that Braille Day was also in November. He said they would appreciate it if you could come that day and participate in the dedication ceremony for the book. You wondered how things had gotten to that point, but you couldn't go back on your "sure." It probably helped that it was early spring, and November seemed far away. But time passed. Spring passed, summer came and went, fall came, and soon enough it was November. And then that day had arrived.

Most things in the world are not unexpected if one thinks carefully about them. Even something one would call unusual—if one thinks about it, it's really just a thing that was supposed to happen. Encountering unusual events often means you didn't think things through. Your trip to the Braille library and the events that occurred there were all things you could have predicted if you'd really thought about the Braille library. But you were busy in the spring, summer, and fall. Even on the day you headed to the Braille library, you weren't thinking about the people you were going to meet there; you were worried that you would be late for the ten o'clock meeting time. You barely made it onto the 8 a.m. flight, then arrived in Pohang, took a cab to the Braille library, and went to the waiting room. The director sat down facing you, with the help of a volunteer. He greeted you politely—"Thank you for coming all this way"—and held his hand out. Trying to mask your nervousness, you shook it, saying brightly, "Hello." His hand was soft. The director talked about your book until right before the event. You smiled and nodded at this blind man who had read your work, even though he couldn't see you smile or nod. That day was Braille Day, their holiday. When you entered the auditorium, four hundred people awaited you, some still trickling in with the help of volunteers. There were men and women of all ages, but no children. The ceremony began, and a few people came to the front, one by one, and made little speeches. Some people received certificates of appreciation. They spoke about your book, and you went to the front to receive the Braille version. Your one book became four volumes in Braille. The books given to you by the director were twice as big as yours, but they were light. You heard applause as you returned to your seat with the books in your hands. The ceremony continued. As plaques were given to congratulate readers, you opened one of the volumes. At once you felt faint. An infinite number of dots on white paper. It was as if you had fallen into a black hole—as if you were walking on stairs you knew so well that climbing them didn't even register in your mind and, while thinking about something else, you missed a step and tumbled down. Braille proliferated the white paper, each letter a hole made by a needle, words you couldn't decipher at all. You told Mom that you'd flipped past the first page and the second page and the third page, and then closed the book. Because your mom was listening intently to your story, you continued.

At the end of the ceremony, you stood in front of everyone and talked about your work. When you laid the books on the dais and looked out at the audience, your back stiffened. You had no idea what to focus on, standing in front of four hundred people who couldn't see.

"So what did you do?" your mom asked.

You told her that the fifty minutes given to you seemed

never-ending. You were the type of person who looked into someone's eyes when you talked. When you talked you sometimes told the entire story, or maybe only half, depending on the feeling you got from the person's eyes. Some eyes coaxed out stories you'd never told anyone. You wondered, Does Mom know that I'm like that? In front of four hundred blind people, you didn't know whom to look at or how to start talking. Some eyes were closed, some half open, and some hidden behind dark glasses; some eyes seemed to stare straight through you and your nervousness. Even though all eyes were aimed at you, you became silent in front of eyes that couldn't see you. You wondered what would be the point of talking about your book in front of these unseeing eyes. But it wasn't appropriate to talk about something else, such as anecdotes from your life. If anything, they should be telling you their life stories. Because you felt stuck, the first thing you said into the mike was "What should I talk about?" They all burst out laughing. Did they laugh because they thought you meant you could tell any story? Or to make you feel more comfortable? A man in his mid-forties replied, "Didn't you come to talk about your work?" The man's eyes were pointed at you but were closed. Focusing on them, you started to talk about the inspiration behind the book, the things you experienced emotionally during its writing, and the hopes you had for the book after you were done. You were surprised. Of all the people you'd met, they listened to your words the most intently. They demonstrated with their bodies that they were listening carefully. One person was nodding, and another pushed one foot forward, and someone else was leaning into the person in front of him. Even though you couldn't understand a word of their writing system, they had read your book and asked questions and shared their thoughts. You told Mom that they revealed such positive feelings about that book, more than anyone else you had encountered. Mom, who was listening quietly, said, "Still, even they've read your book." A short silence flowed between you and Mom. Mom asked you to go on. You continued.

When you stopped talking, one person raised his hand and asked if he could ask a question. You told him to go ahead. "Even though he's blind, he said traveling was his hobby, Mom." You were stunned. Where would a blind person travel? He said he'd read something you had written a long time ago that was based in Peru. The character in the novel went to Machu Picchu, and there was a scene where a train went backward. He said after he read that he wanted to ride that train in Peru. He asked if you had personally ridden the train. It was a work you had written over ten years ago. You, who had such a bad memory that you often opened the refrigerator door and forgot why you had opened it, and would stand there for a while with the chill of the fridge washing over you until you gave up and shut the door, started to talk about Peru, where you had traveled before you wrote that book. Lima; Cuzco, dubbed the Belly Button of the Universe; San Pedro Station, where you took the train to Machu Picchu at dawn. About the train that started forward and jerked backward many times before starting off to Machu Picchu. You told Mom, "The names of the places and mountains that I'd forgotten about poured out." Feeling friendship from eyes that had never seen, eyes that seemed to understand and accept any flaw of yours, you said something you had never said about that book. Mom asked, "What was it?"

"I said if I were to write it again I don't think I would write it like that."

"Is that such a big deal to say?" she asked.

"Yes, because I was rejecting what exists, Mom!"

Mom gazed at you in the darkness and said, "Why do you hide those words? You have to live free, saying whatever you feel," and pulled her hand from your grasp and rubbed your back. When you were a child, she used to wash your face the same way, with her big soothing hands. "You tell such good stories," she said.

"Me?"

Mom nodded. "Yeah, I liked it."

She liked my story? You were moved. You knew that what you'd said wasn't all that good; it was just that you were talking to her differently after your experience at the Braille library. After you'd left home for the city, you'd always talked to her as if you were angry at her. You talked back to her, saying, "What do you know, Mom?" "Why would you do that, as a mother?" you'd rebuke. "Why do you want to know?" you retorted coldly. After you figured out that Mom no longer had the power to scold you, if she asked, "Why are you going there?" you replied curtly, "Because I have to." Even when you had to take a plane because your book was being published in another country, or you had to go abroad for a seminar, when she asked, "Why are you going there?" you stiffly replied, "Because I have business to take care of." Mom told you to stop taking airplanes. "If there's an accident, two hundred people die at once." "It's because I have work to do," you'd say. If Mom asked, "Why do you have so much work?" you replied, sullenly, "Yes, all right, Mom." It was difficult to talk to her about your life, which had nothing to do with hers. But when you talked about feeling lost seeing the Braille version of your book, and the mounting panic you felt standing in front of four hundred blind people, she listened as intently as if her headache had gone away. When was the last time you'd told Mom about something that had happened to you? At a certain point, the conversations between you and Mom became simplified. Even that was not done face to face, but by telephone. Your words had to do with whether she ate, whether she was healthy, how Father was, that she should be careful not to catch cold, that you were sending money. Mom talked about how she made kimchi and sent some, that she had strange dreams, that she sent rice, or fermented bean paste, that she'd brewed motherwort to send you, and that you shouldn't turn off your phone because the messenger would call before delivering all these packages.

———

Carrying a paper bag that held your Braille books, you said goodbye to the people at the Braille library. You still had two hours to kill before your return flight. You remembered standing at the dais and looking out the window, averting your gaze from those blind eyes, and seeing the harbor dotted with boats. You thought, Well, since there's a harbor, there's got to be a fish market. You took a cab and asked to be taken there. You like to visit the market whenever you have time to spare in a place you've never been. Even on a weekday, the fish market was bustling. Outside the market you saw two people cutting apart a fish that was as big as a sedan. You asked if it was tuna, since it was so large, but the vendor said it was an ocean sunfish. You were reminded of a character in a book whose title you couldn't remember. She was from a seaside town, and she would go to the huge aquarium in the city every time she had a problem, to talk to the ocean sunfish swimming inside. She would complain that her mother took all her life savings and went off with a younger man to a different city, but then, at the end, would say, But I miss my mom; you're the only one I can tell this to, sunfish! You wondered if that was the same fish. Thinking it was a unique name for a fish, you asked, "Really, it's called an ocean sunfish?" And the vendor said, "We also call it Mola mola!" As soon as you heard the words "Mola mola," the tension you had been feeling inside the library dissipated. Why did you think of Mom as you wandered among the heaps of seafood, which cost a third of what they did in Seoul: live octopus with heads bigger than a human's, fresh abalone, scabbard fish, mackerel, and crab? Was it the ocean sunfish that made you think of Mom for the first time at a fish market? That made you recall preparing skate at home, by the well, next to Mom? You could see Mom's frozen hands peeling the brownish mucus stuck to the meat. You stopped at a store that had a boiled octopus as big as a child's torso hanging from the ceiling and bought a live octopus for fifteen thousand won. You bought some abalone—though they were farm-raised, they had been fed different kinds of seaweed. When you said you were going to Seoul, the vendor offered to put your purchase in an ice chest for an extra two thousand won. As you walked out of the fish market, you realized you still had a lot of time left before your flight. Holding the Braille volumes in one hand and the ice chest in the other, you hopped into another cab and told the driver that you wanted to go to the beach. It took only three minutes to get there. The November beach was empty except for two couples. The beach was big. As you walked toward the water, you almost fell twice. You sat down on the fine sand and stared at the sea. After a while, you turned around to look at the stores and apartment buildings facing the ocean across the road. People who lived here could jump into the ocean on a hot night, then go home and take a shower. You absent-mindedly took out a Braille volume from the paper bag and opened it. The white dots on the pages sparkled in the sunlight.

Tracing your finger along the indecipherable Braille in the sun, you wondered who had taught you to read. It was your second-eldest brother. The two of you lying on your stomachs on the porch of the old house. Mom sitting next to you. Your brother, a gentle soul, caused the least trouble among your siblings. Unable to disobey Mom's orders to teach you how to read, his expression bored, he directed you to write numbers and vowels and consonants over and over. You tried to write with your dominant left hand. Every time, your brother rapped the back of your hand with a bamboo ruler. He was doing Mom's bidding. Even though it was more natural for you to favor your left hand and foot, Mom told you that there would be many things to cry about in life if you used your left hand. When you used your left hand to scoop rice in the kitchen, Mom wrenched the scoop out of your hand and put it in your right hand. If you tried to use your left hand anyway, she would grab the scoop and slap your left hand, saying, "Why won't you listen to me?" Your left hand became swollen. Even so, when your brother wasn't watching, you quickly switched the pencil to your left hand and drew two circles, one on top of the other, for the "8." Then you switched the pencil back to your right. Your brother, who knew that you had stuck together two circles as soon as he saw your "8," told you to put your palms out and slapped them with the ruler. As you were learning how to read, Mom looked over your crouched form on the porch, while she mended socks or peeled garlic. When you learned to write your name and Mom's name and read books hesitantly before enrolling in school, your mom's face bloomed like a mint flower. That face overlapped with the Braille you couldn't read.

You stood up and hurried back to the road without bothering to brush the sand off your clothes. You decided against taking the plane to Seoul, and instead took a taxi to Taejon and got on a train to Chongup. Thinking all the while that you hadn't seen Mom's face in almost two seasons.

———

You remember a classroom from long ago.

It was a day that the sixty or so kids filled out applications for middle school. If you didn't write an application that day, you were not going to middle school. You were one of the kids not working on an application. You didn't completely understand what it meant that you would not be going on to middle school. Instead, you were feeling guilty.

The night before, Mom had yelled at Father, who was sick in bed. She had shouted at him, "We don't have anything, so how is that girl going to survive in this world if we don't send her to school?" Father got up and left the house, and Mom lifted a squat table from the floor and threw it into the yard in frustration. "What's the point of having a household when you can't even send your kids to school? I might as well break it all!" You wished she would calm down; you didn't mind not going to school. Mom wasn't appeased by throwing the table. She opened and banged shut the door of the cellar and yanked all the laundry off the line, crumpled it, and threw it on the ground. Then she came to you, cowering by the well, and took the towel off her head and brought it to your nose. She ordered, "Blow your nose." You could smell the intense stink of sweat on Mom's towel. You didn't want to blow your nose, especially not into that smelly towel. But Mom kept telling you to blow your nose as hard as you could. When you hesitated, she said that way you wouldn't cry. You were probably standing there looking at Mom with an expression bordering on tears. Telling you to blow your nose was her way of saying, Don't cry. Unable to resist her, you blew your nose, and your snot and the smell of sweat mingled in the towel.

Mom came to school the next day wearing that same towel. After she spoke with your teacher, your teacher came to you and handed you an application form. You raised your head and looked outside the classroom as you wrote your name on the form, and you saw Mom watching you from the hall. When your eyes met, she took the towel off her head and waved it, smiling brightly.

Around the time the fee for middle school was due, the gold ring that used to be on Mom's left middle finger, her sole piece of jewelry, disappeared from her hand. Only the groove on her finger, etched by many years of wearing the band, was left behind.

———

Headaches attacked Mom's body constantly.

During that visit to your childhood home, you woke up thirsty in the middle of the night and saw your books looming over you in the dark. You hadn't known what to do with all of your books when you prepared to go to Japan for a year with Yu-bin on his sabbatical. You sent most of the books, books that had stayed with you for years, to your parents' house. As soon as Mom received your books, she emptied out a room and displayed them there. After that, you never found the opportunity to take them back with you. When you visited your parents' house, you used that room to change your clothes or to store your bags, and if you stayed over, that was where Mom would place your blankets and sleeping mat.

After you got a drink of water and returned to your room, you wondered how Mom was sleeping, and you carefully pushed her door open. It looked as if she wasn't there. "Mom!" you called. No answer. You fumbled with the switch on the wall and turned on the light. Mom wasn't there. You turned on the light in the living room and opened the bathroom door, but she wasn't there, either. "Mom! Mom!" you called as you pushed the front door open and stepped into the yard. The early-morning wind burrowed into your clothes. You turned on the light in the yard and glanced quickly at the wooden platform in the shed. Mom was lying there. You ran down the steps to the yard and approached her. She was frowning, as she had done earlier, asleep, hand on her head. She was barefoot, and her toes were curled under, perhaps from the cold. The simple dinner and the talk you had shared while you strolled around the house together shattered. It was an early morning in November. You brought out a blanket and covered Mom with it. You brought socks and put them on her feet. And you sat next to her until she woke up.

———

Thinking of ways to earn money other than from farming, Mom brought a wooden malt-mold into the shed. She would take the whole wheat she harvested from the fields and crush it and mix it with water and put it in the mold and make malt. When the malt fermented, the entire house smelled of it.

Nobody liked that smell, but Mom said it was the smell of money. There was a house in the village where they made tofu, and when she brought them the fermented malt, they sold it to the brewery and gave the money to Mom. Mom put that money in a white bowl, stacked six or seven bowls on top of it, and placed it on top of the cabinets. The bowl was Mom's bank. She put all her money up there. When you brought home the invoice for tuition, she took money from the bowl, counted it out, and put it in your hand.

———

Later in the morning, when you again opened your eyes, you discovered that you were lying on the platform in the shed. Where was Mom? She wasn't there, but you could hear chopping from the kitchen. You got up and went in. Mom was about to slice a large, white radish on the chopping block. The way she held the knife looked precarious. It wasn't the way she used to julienne radish to make slaw, expertly, without looking down. Mom's hand holding the knife was unstable, and the knife kept slipping off the radish onto the chopping block. It seemed she would cut her thumb off. "Mom! Wait!" You grabbed the knife from her hand. "I'll do it, Mom." You moved to the chopping block. Mom paused but then stepped aside. The steel basket in the sink held the languid, dead octopus. There was a stainless-steel steamer on the gas range. She was going to put a layer of radish on the bottom of the steamer and steam the octopus. You were about to ask, Aren't you supposed to parboil the octopus, not steam it? But you didn't.

Mom arranged slices of radish on the bottom of the steamer and adjusted a stainless-steel shelf inside. She put the whole octopus in and placed the lid on top. This was the way she usually cooked seafood.

Mom wasn't used to fish. She didn't even call fish by their proper names. To Mom, mackerel and pike and scabbard fish were all just fish. But she differentiated between types of beans: kidney beans, soybeans, white beans, black beans. When Mom had fish in her kitchen, she never made sashimi or broiled or braised it, but always salted and steamed it. Even for mackerel or scabbard fish, she made a soy-based sauce with red-pepper flakes, garlic, and pepper and steamed it on a plate over rice that was cooking. Mom never put sashimi in her mouth. When she saw people eating raw fish, she looked at them with a distasteful expression that said, What are they doing? Mom, who had steamed skate from the time she was seventeen years old, wanted to steam octopus, too. Soon the kitchen was filled with the smell of radish and octopus. As you watched Mom steaming octopus in the kitchen, you thought of skate.

People from Mom's region always put skate on their ancestral-rite table. Mom's year was structured around the ancestral rites she held, once in spring and twice each in summer and winter. Mom had to sit next to a well and clean seven skates each year, if one counted New Year's and Full Moon Harvest. Usually the skate Mom bought was as big as a cauldron lid. When your mom went to the market and bought a red skate and dropped it next to the well, this meant that an ancestral rite was approaching. It was hard work to clean skate for the winter ancestral rites, in weather that instantly turned water into ice. Your hands were small, and Mom's were thickened from labor. When Mom made a slit with the knife in the skin of the skate with her red, frozen hands, your young fingers pulled the membranes off. It would have been easier if they came off in one piece, but they would fall off in sections. Mom would make another slit in the fish, and the whole process would be repeated. It was a typical winter scene, you and your mom squatting by the well that was covered in thin ice, skinning the skate. The cleaning of the skate repeated itself each year, as if someone were rewinding film. One winter, Mom gazed at your frozen hands as you sat across from her and declared, "Who cares if we don't skin it," stopped what she was doing, and confidently cut the fish into chunks. It was the first time that the ancestral-rite table had seen a skate with its skin on. Father asked, "What's wrong with this skate?" Mom replied, "It's the same skate, just not skinned." Father's sister grumbled, "You have to put care into food for the ancestral rites." "Then you try peeling it," Mom retorted. That year, whenever something bad happened, someone brought up the unpeeled skate. When the persimmon tree didn't bear fruit; when one of your brothers, who was playing a stick-toss game, got poked in the eye by a flying stick; when Father was hospitalized; when cousins fought—Father's sister grumbled that it was because Mom hadn't bothered to skin the skate for the ancestral rites.

Mom placed the steamed octopus on the chopping block and tried to slice it. But the knife kept slipping, just as it had when she was slicing the radish. "I'll do it, Mom." You took her knife again, sliced the hot radish-scented octopus, dipped a piece in red-pepper-and-vinegar sauce, and held it out to Mom. This was what she'd always done for you. Each time, you'd tried to pick it up in the air with your own chopsticks, but Mom would say, "If you eat it with your chopsticks, it doesn't taste as good. Just open your mouth." Now Mom tried to lift it in the air with her own chopsticks, and you said, "If you do that it won't taste as good, just open your mouth." You pushed the piece of octopus into her mouth. You tried one, too. The octopus was warm and squishy and soft. You wondered, Octopus for breakfast? But you and Mom ate it with your fingers, standing in the kitchen. As you chewed on the octopus, you watched Mom's hand as she tried to pick up a piece and dropped it. You put a piece in her mouth for her. Soon she gave up trying to eat the octopus herself and waited for you to plop it in her mouth. Her hand seemed unfocused. Eating the octopus, you said, "Mother." It was the first time you had called her "Mother." "Mother, let's go to Seoul today." Your mom replied, "Let's go up into the mountains."

"The mountains?"

"Yeah, the mountains."

"Is there a hiking trail from here?"

"I've made one myself."

"Let's go to Seoul and go to the hospital there."

"Later."

"Later when?"

"When your niece's entrance exam is over." She was referring to Hyong-chol's daughter.

"You can go to the hospital with me instead of with Hyong-chol."

"I'm fine. It'll be fine. I'm going to the doctor of Chinese medicine for it. I'm getting physical therapy, too, because they said something's wrong with my neck."

You couldn't persuade Mom—she kept insisting that she would go later. Then she asked you what the world's smallest country was.

The smallest country? You stared at Mom, a stranger asking you a random question: What is the smallest country in the world? Mom asked you to get rose rosary beads for her if you ever went to that country.

"Rose rosary beads?"

"Prayer beads made of rosewood." She looked at you listlessly.

"Do you need prayer beads?"

"No, I just want prayer beads from that country." Mom stopped and let out a deep sigh. "If you ever go there, get me a set."

You were quiet.

"Because you can go anywhere."

Your conversation with Mom stopped there. She didn't say another word in the kitchen. After the breakfast of steamed octopus, you and your mom left the house. You went across a few paddies in the mountains that rimmed the back of the village and stepped onto a trail in the hills. Even though it wasn't a path people used, the trail was clear. The thick layers of oak leaves on the ground cushioned your feet. Sometimes the branches that reached into the trail hit your face. Mom, who was ahead of you, pushed the branches back for you. She let go of them after you walked through. A bird flew away.

"Do you come here often?"

"Yes."

"With who?"

"Nobody. There's nobody who would come with me."

Mom walked this path by herself? You really couldn't say you knew Mom. It was a dark path for anyone to walk alone. At some parts, the bamboos were so dense that you couldn't see the sky.

"Why do you walk here by yourself?"

"I came here once after your aunt died, and I kept coming back."

After a while, Mom stopped on top of a hill. When you came up next to her and looked where she was looking, you shouted, "Oh, this path!" It was a path you had completely forgotten about, the shortcut to your mom's mother's house, which you used to take when you were young. Even after they built the big road that passed through the village, people often used this mountain trail. It was the path you had taken one day when your grandmother was busy preparing for her ancestral rites, a live chicken trailing behind you on a rope. You had dropped the rope and lost the chicken. Though you had looked for it everywhere, you weren't able to find it. Where had that chicken gone? Had the trail changed so much? You used to be able to walk this path with your eyes closed, but now, if it weren't for the hill, you wouldn't have known it was the same path. Mom stood there, staring at the place where her mother's house once stood. Nobody lived there anymore. The people from that village, which once must have numbered fifty households, had all moved away. A few empty houses hadn't been torn down, but it was a village that people had stopped coming to. So Mom had come here by herself to look down at the empty village she was born in? You wrapped your arm around her waist, and suggested again that she come to Seoul with you. Mom didn't reply, and instead brought up the dog. You had been curious when you first noticed that the dog wasn't in the doghouse, but you hadn't had a chance to ask.

A year before, when you'd gone home in the summer, there was a Chindo tied next to the shed. It was sweltering, and the chain was so short that it seemed the panting dog, unable to get out of the sun, would fall over dead at any moment. You told Mom to untie the dog. Mom said that if she did people would be too scared to walk by. How could she chain a dog up like that, especially in the countryside . . . Because of the dog, you argued with Mom as soon as you arrived, not even bothering to say hello. "Why do you keep the dog tied up? Let it roam." But Mom insisted, "Nobody, not even in the country, lets their dog run around. Everyone ties their dog on a chain—if you don't, it'll get lost." You shot back, "Then you have to get a longer chain. If you tie it up with such a short chain, how is a dog supposed to survive in this heat? Do you treat it like that just because it can't speak up for itself?" Mom said that was the only chain in the house; it was the one she had used for the previous dog. "Then you can go buy one!" Even though you'd come home for the first time in a long while, you drove back to town before setting foot in the house and brought back a chain so long that the dog could wander down the side yard. That's when you realized the dog-house was small. You headed out again, saying you were going to get another doghouse. But Mom stopped you, insisting that there was a carpenter in a neighboring village whom she could ask to build her a new doghouse. Your mom couldn't fathom paying for a house for an animal: "There are pieces of wood everywhere, and all you need to do is hammer it here and there, and you want to pay money for that? You must have money rotting in your pockets." Later, when you left for the city, you gave her two ten-thousand-won checks and got her to promise that she would build the dog a big house. Mom promised she would. Back in Seoul, you called a few times to make sure that Mom had the doghouse built. Though she could have lied, each time she said, "I'm going to, I'll do it soon." The fourth time you called and heard the same answer, your anger overflowed.

"I gave you the money for it and everything. Country people are terrible. Don't you feel bad for the dog? How is it supposed to live in that tiny space, especially in this heat? There's feces inside, and the poor thing has stepped all over it, and you don't even clean it up. How can such a big dog live in such a small contraption? Otherwise, let him roam free in the yard! Don't you feel bad for the dog?"

The phone went silent. You started to regret saying that country people were terrible.

Mom's angry voice came shooting across the line. "You care only about the dog, and not your own mother? Do you think your mother is the kind of person who would abuse a

dog? Don't tell me what to do! I'm going to raise it my way!"
Mom hung up first.

You were the one who always hung up first. You would
say, "Mom, I'll call you back," and then you didn't. You didn't
have time to sit and listen to everything your mom had to say.
But this time your mom had hung up on you. It was the first
time Mom had gotten so angry with you since you left home.
Once you moved out, Mom always said, "I'm sorry." She con-
fessed that she'd sent you to live with Hyong-chol because she
couldn't take care of you well enough. Mom would try as hard
as she could to lengthen the call when you phoned. But even
though she hung up first, you were more disappointed in the
way she was keeping the dog. You were puzzled. How had
Mom become that person? She used to look after all the animals in the house. She was the kind of person who would come
to Seoul for an extended stay and three days later insist on
going home to feed the dog. How could she be so clueless now?
You were annoyed at your mom for becoming so insensitive.

A few days later, Mom called. "You weren't like this
before, but you've become cold. If your mother hangs up like
that, you're supposed to call her back. How could you dig in
your heels?"

It wasn't that you had been stubborn; you hadn't had time
to think about it for that long. You would remember how
Mom had hung up, angry, and think, I should give her a call,
but because of one thing or another you would push calling
her to the end of your list.

"Are all educated people like this?" Mom snapped, and
hung up.

Around Full Moon Harvest, you went to your parents' house and saw that there was a big doghouse next to the shed. On the floor of the doghouse was a soft layer of hay.

Standing next to you on the hill, your mom started talking. "In October, while I was washing rice at the sink to make breakfast, someone kept tapping me on the back. When I looked around, nobody was there. It was like that for three whole days: I felt something tapping me, as if they were calling me, but nobody was there when I looked. It must have been the fourth day; as soon as I woke up, I went to the bathroom, and the dog was lying in front of the toilet. You got angry with me last year, saying that I was abusing the dog, but that dog had been wandering around the railroad tracks, covered with mange. I felt bad for him, so I brought him home and tied him up and gave him food. If you don't tie him up, you don't know where he'll go, or whether someone's going to catch him and eat him. . . . That day, he didn't move. At first I thought he was sleeping. He didn't move even when I nudged him. He was dead. He'd been eating well and wagging his tail the day before, but he was dead, and he looked peaceful. I don't know how he got loose from the chain. At first he was all bones. He'd fattened up, and his coat was getting shiny. And he was so smart. He would catch moles." Mom paused to sigh. "They say that if you take in a person he will betray you, and if you take in a dog he will pay you back. I think the dog went in my place."

This time you sighed.

"Last spring, I donated money to a passing monk and he

said that this year one member in our family would be gone. When I heard that, I was anxious. For an entire year I thought of that. I think death came to fetch me, but because I was washing rice to cook for myself every time, he took the dog instead."

"Mom, what are you talking about? How can you believe that, when you go to church?" You thought of the empty doghouse next to the shed, and the chain on the ground. You put an arm around Mom's waist.

"I dug a deep grave in the yard and buried him."

Your mom always did tell imaginative stories. On the night of an ancestral rite, Father's sister and other aunts would come over with bowls of rice. It was when food was scarce, so they would all contribute. After the ancestral rites, your mom would fill the relatives' bowls with food for them to take home. During the rites, the bowls of rice sat in a row nearby; afterward, Mom said that birds had flown in and perched on the rice, then left. If you didn't believe her, she'd say, "I saw them! There were six birds. The birds are our ancestors, who came to eat!" The others laughed, but you thought you could see their footprints in the white rice. Once, Mom went to the fields in the early morning, bringing along a snack for later, but someone was there already, bent over and pulling weeds. When she asked who he was, he said he was passing by and stopped to pull weeds because there were so many. Mom and the stranger weeded together. She was grateful, so she shared the snack she had brought. They talked about this and that and weeded the field and went their separate ways when it got dark. When she came back from the field and told Father's sister that she had weeded with the stranger, Father's sister stiffened and asked what he looked like. "That used to be the owner of that field. He died of sunstroke one day while he was weeding the field." You asked, "Mom, weren't you scared to be in the field with a dead person all day?" But your mom replied nonchalantly, "I wasn't scared. If I'd had to weed that field all by myself, it would have taken two or three days. So I'm just grateful he helped me."

———

After your visit, you noticed how your mom's headaches seemed to be eating away at her. She quickly lost her outgoing personality and vivacity, and started to lie down more often. Your mom couldn't even concentrate on card games with hundred-won bets, which were among the few joys in her life. And her senses became dull. One day, after she put a pot of rags on the gas range to bleach them, your mom crumpled on the floor of the kitchen and couldn't get back up. All the water evaporated, the rags began to burn, and the kitchen was enveloped in smoke, but your mom couldn't snap out of it. The house might have gone up in flames if a neighbor hadn't come in to see what was going on, after catching a glimpse of the column of smoke in the air.

Your sister, who has three kids, once asked you a question about your mom and her constant headaches: "Do you think Mom liked being in the kitchen?" Her voice was low, serious.

"Why do you ask?"

"Somehow I don't think she did."

Your sister, who was a pharmacist, opened her pharmacy while pregnant with her first child. Your sister-in-law babysat for the infant, but she lived far from the pharmacy. The baby lived with your sister-in-law for a while. Your sister, who'd always loved children, ran the pharmacy even though she could see her baby only once a week. It was wrenching to watch her part with her baby. There couldn't have been a farewell as sorrowful as that. But your sister seemed to have more trouble with the situation than the baby. While he adapted to his life away from his mother fairly well, she drove him back to your sister-in-law's at the end of each weekend crying, her tears drenching her hands as they gripped the steering wheel on the way home, and on Monday she stood in her pharmacy with her eyes swollen from weeping. It was so bad that you would say, "Do you really need to go to such lengths to run a pharmacy?" When your sister's husband was to go to the United States for two years of training, your sister closed the pharmacy, which she had continued to run even after she had her second child. She said she thought living in America would be a good experience for the kids, and you thought, Yes, please take it easy and take some time off. She had never once taken time off after she got married. She had her third baby in the States and then returned. Now she had to cook for a family of five. Your sister said that once they ate two hundred croakers in one month.

"Two hundred in one month? Did you only eat croakers?" you asked, and she said they had.

This was before their things had arrived from America, and she wasn't used to the new house yet, and the newborn was still breastfeeding, so there wasn't time to go to the market. Her mother-in-law sent a chest of baby croakers, salted and gently dried, and they ate the whole thing in ten days. Your sister laughed and said, "I would make bean-sprout soup and broil a couple of fish, then make zucchini soup and fish." When she asked her mother-in-law where she could get more, she found out that she could order them online. Because they had eaten through the first batch so quickly, she ordered two.

"When the croakers came, I washed them and counted; there were two hundred. I was washing the fish so that I could wrap four or five of them in plastic and put them in the freezer, to make them easier to cook, and all of a sudden I wanted to fling them all on the floor," your sister said calmly. "And I thought of Mom. I wondered, How did Mom feel all those years in that old-fashioned kitchen, cooking for our big family? Remember how much we ate? We had two small tables filled with food. Remember how big our rice pot was? And she had to pack all of our lunches, including the side dishes she made with whatever she could get in the countryside. . . . How did Mom get through it every day? Since Father was the eldest, there was always a relative or two staying with us. I don't think Mom could have liked being in the kitchen at all."

You were caught off guard. You had never thought of Mom as separate from the kitchen. Mom was the kitchen and the kitchen was Mom. You never wondered, Did Mom like being in the kitchen?

———

To earn money, your mom bred silkworms and brewed malt and helped make tofu. The best way to make money was not to use it. Mom saved everything. Sometimes she would sell a ratty lamp, a worn ironing stone, or an old jar to people from out of town. They wanted the antiques that Mom was using, and even though she wasn't attached to any of those things, she haggled with people over the price as if she had become a vendor. At first it would seem your mom was losing, but then she would get her way. After listening to them quietly, she'd say, "Then just give me this amount," and they would scoff, "Who would buy that useless thing for so much?" Mom would retort, "Then why do you go around buying this stuff?" and take the lamp back. They would grumble, "You'd make a good merchant," and give Mom what she asked for.

Your mom never paid full price for anything. Most things she did herself, so her hands were always busy. She sewed and knitted, and she tilled the fields without rest. Mom's fields were never empty. In the spring she planted potato seeds in furrows and planted lettuce and crown daisies and mallow and garlic chives and peppers and corn. Under the fence around the house she dug holes for zucchini, and in the field she planted beans. Mom was always growing sesame and mulberry leaves and cucumbers. She was either in the kitchen or in the fields or in the paddies. She plucked potatoes and yams and zucchini, and pulled cabbages and radishes from the ground. Mom's labor showed that nothing would be reaped if the seeds were not sown. She paid only for things that could not be grown from seeds: ducklings or chicks that ran around in the yard in the spring, piglets that lived in the sty.

One year the dog gave birth to nine puppies. After a month passed, Mom left two behind and put six in a basket and, because the basket was full, put the last one in your arms. "Follow me," she said. The bus you and Mom rode was crowded with people who were going into town to sell things: sacks of dried pepper and sesame and black beans; baskets weighed down with just a few cabbages and radishes. Everyone huddled in a row at the township bus stop, and passersby stopped to strike a deal. You slipped the warm puppy you were holding into the basket with the other squirming puppies, squatted next to Mom, and waited for them to be sold. The puppies, which Mom had taken care of for a month, were plump and healthy, gentle, without any suspicion or hostility toward people. They wagged their tails at the people who gathered around the basket and licked their hands. Mom's puppies sold faster than the radishes or the cabbages or the beans. When she sold the last one, she stood up and asked, "What do you want?" You held on to her hand and stared at her, your mom, who had rarely asked you such a thing.

"I said, what do you want?"

"A book!"

"A book?"

"Yeah, a book!"

Mom acted as if she didn't know what to do. She looked down at you for a minute and asked where they sold books. You took the lead and guided Mom to the bookstore at the entrance of the market, where five roads met. Mom didn't go in. "Pick out just one," she said, "and ask how much it is and come tell me." Even when she bought rubber shoes, she made you try on each one, and always ended up paying less than what the shopkeeper wanted; but for a book she told you to pick one, as if she wasn't going to haggle over the price. The bookstore suddenly felt like a prairie to you. You had no idea which book to choose. The reason you wanted a book was that you would read books your brothers brought home from school, but they always took the books away from you before you read them to the end. The school library had different books from the ones that Hyong-chol brought home. Books like *Mrs. Sa Goes to the South* or *Biography of Shin Yun-bok*. The book you chose, while Mom stood outside the bookstore, was *Human, All Too Human*. Mom, about to pay for a book that wasn't a textbook for the first time in her life, looked down at the book you'd picked out.

"Is this a book you need?"

You nodded quickly, worried that she would change her mind. Actually, you didn't know what this book was. It said that it was written by Nietzsche, but you didn't know who that was. You'd just picked it because you liked the way the title sounded. Mom gave you the money for the book, the full price. On the bus, clasping the book against your chest instead of the puppy, you gazed out the window. You saw an old, stooped woman looking at passersby desperately, trying to sell the bowlful of sticky rice that remained in her rubber bin.

———

On the mountain path where you could see your grandparents' old village, your mom told you that her father, who drifted from town to town, digging for gold and coal, came home when she was three years old. He went to work at a construction site for a new train station and got in an accident. Villagers who came to tell Grandmother about the accident looked at Mom, running and playing in the yard, and said, "You're laughing even though your father has died, you silly child."

"You remember that from when you were three?"

"I do."

Your mom said she was sometimes resentful of her mom, your grandmother. "I'm sure she had to do everything herself as a widow, but she should have sent me to school. My brother went to a Japanese-run school, and my sister did, too, so why did she keep me at home? I lived in darkness, with no light, my entire life. . . ."

Your mom finally agreed to come to Seoul with you if you promised not to tell Hyong-chol. Even when she left the house with you, she kept asking you to promise this.

As you went from hospital to hospital to find the source of Mom's headaches, a doctor told you something surprising: your mom had had a stroke a long time ago. A stroke? You said that had never happened. The doctor pointed at a spot on her brain scan and said it was evidence of a stroke. "How could she have had a stroke without even knowing about it?" The doctor said your mom would have known. Given how the blood was pooled there, she would have felt the shock. The doctor said Mom was in constant pain. That Mom's body was in constant pain.

"What do you mean, in constant pain? Mom has always been pretty healthy."

"Well, I don't think that's true," the doctor said.

You felt as if a nail hidden in your pocket had leaped out and ambushed you, stabbing the back of your hand. The doctor drained the blood pooled in Mom's brain, but her headaches didn't get better. One minute Mom would be talking, and the next minute she would be holding her head gingerly, as if it were a glass jar about to break, and she would have to go home and lie down on the wooden platform in the shed.

————

"Mom, do you like being in the kitchen?" When you asked this once, your mom didn't understand what you meant.

"Did you like being in the kitchen? Did you like to cook?"

Mom's eyes held yours for a moment. "I don't like or dislike the kitchen. I cooked because I had to. I had to stay in the kitchen so you could all eat and go to school. How could you only do what you like? There are things you have to do whether you like it or not." Mom's expression asked, What kind of question is that? And then she murmured, "If you only do what you like, who's going to do what you don't like?"

"So—what—you liked it or not?"

Mom looked around, as if she was going to tell you a secret, and whispered, "I broke jar lids several times."

"You broke jar lids?"

"I couldn't see an end to it. At least with farming, if you plant seeds in the spring you harvest them in the fall. If you plant spinach seeds, there is spinach; where you plant corn, there's corn. . . . But there's no beginning or end to kitchen work. You eat breakfast, then it's lunch, and then it's dinner, and when it's bright again it's breakfast again. . . . It might have been better if I could have made different side dishes, but since the same things were planted in the fields, I always made the same panchan. If you do that over and over, there are times when you get so sick of it. When the kitchen felt like a prison, I went out to the back and picked up the most misshapen jar lid and threw it as hard as I could at the wall. Aunt doesn't know that I did that. If she did, she would say I was crazy, throwing jar lids around."

Your mom told you that she would buy a new lid within a few days to replace the one she broke. "So I wasted some money. When I went to get the new lid, I thought it was so wasteful and felt terrible, but I couldn't stop. The sound of the lid breaking was medicine to me. I felt free." Your mom put a finger to her lips and said, "Shh," in case someone could hear. "It's the first time I'm telling this to anyone!" A mischievous grin hovered on her face. "If you don't want to cook, you should try throwing a dish. Even if you're thinking, Oh, what a waste, you're going to feel so light. Of course, since you're not married, you wouldn't feel that way anyway."

Your mom let out a deep sigh. "But it was nice when you kids were growing up. Even when I was so busy that I didn't have time to retie the towel on my head, when I watched you sitting around the table, eating, with your spoons making a racket in the bowls, I felt like there was nothing else I wanted in the world. You were all so easy. You dug in happily when I made a simple zucchini-and-bean-paste soup, and your faces lit up if I steamed some fish once in a while. . . . You were all such good eaters that when you were growing I was some-times afraid. If I left a pot filled with boiled potatoes for your after-school snack, the pot would be empty when I came home. And there were days when I could see the rice in the jar in the cellar disappearing day by day, and times when the jar would be empty. When I went to the cellar to get some rice for dinner and my scoop scraped the bottom of the rice jar, my heart would sink: What am I going to feed my babies tomor-row morning? So in those days it wasn't about whether I liked to be in the kitchen or not. If I made a big pot of rice and a smaller pot of soup, I didn't think of how tired I was. I felt good that these were going into my babies' mouths. Now, you probably can't even imagine it, but in those days we were always worried that we would run out of food. We were all like that. The most important thing was eating and surviv-ing." Smiling, your mom told you that those days were the happiest in her life.

. . .

But Mom's headaches stole the smiles from her face. Her headaches jabbed at her soul and slowly ate away at it, like field mice with sharp teeth.

———

The man you went to for help in printing the flyers is wearing old cotton clothes. Anyone glancing at him would be able to tell that he's wearing a very carefully sewn outfit. Even though you know he always wears old cotton clothes, you can't help focusing on them. He has already heard about your mom and tells you that he will design the flyer based on your mock-up and print them out quickly, at a printing shop his business acquaintance uses. Since there aren't any recent pictures of Mom, you and your siblings have decided to use the family picture that your brother posted on the Internet. The man looks at Mom's face in the picture. "Your mother is very pretty," he says.

Out of the blue, you comment that his clothes are very nice.

He smiles at your words. "My mother made this for me."

"But didn't she pass away?"

"When she was alive."

He tells you that since he was a child he has only been able to wear cotton, because of various allergies. When other fabrics touched his skin, he became itchy and got a rash. He grew up wearing only the cotton clothes his mother made. In his memories, his mother was always sewing. She would have had to sew and sew to make everything personally, from his underwear to his socks.

He says that when he opened her closet after she passed away he found stacks of cotton clothes that would last him for the rest of his life. That his outfit today is one he found in that closet. What did his mother look like? Your heart aches as you listen to him. You ask the man who is remembering his beloved mother, "Do you think your mother was happy?"

His words are polite, but his expression tells you that you've insulted his mother:

"My mother was different from today's women."

2

I'm Sorry, Hyong-chol

A WOMAN TAKES ONE of his flyers and pauses for a moment to look at the picture of Mom. Under the clock tower where Mom used to wait for him.

After he found a place in the city, Mom would arrive at Seoul Station looking like a war refugee. She would walk onto the platform with bundles balanced on her head and slung over her shoulders and in her hands, the things she couldn't otherwise carry strapped to her waist. It was amazing that she could still walk. If she could have, Mom would have come to see him with eggplants or pumpkins tied to her legs. Her pockets often bulged with unripe peppers, peeled chestnuts, or peeled garlic wrapped in newspaper. Whenever he went to meet her, he would see a heap of so many parcels by Mom's feet and marvel that one woman could have brought them all by herself. Standing amid the packages, Mom would look around, her cheeks flushed, waiting for him.

The woman comes up to him hesitantly, pointing to the picture of his mom printed on the flyer, and says, "Excuse me, I think I've seen her in front of the Yongsan 2-dong office." On the flyer his younger sister made, his mom smiles brightly, wearing a pale-blue hanbok. The woman continues, "She wasn't wearing this outfit, but the eyes are so similar, and I remember them because they looked honest and loyal." The woman looks again at his mom's eyes in the flyer and adds, "She had a cut on her foot." She says his mom was wearing blue plastic sandals, one of which was cutting into her foot near her big toe, and a piece of flesh had fallen off, creating a groove, perhaps because she'd walked so far. The woman tells him that flies buzzed around and landed near the pus-filled wound, and that his mom kept shooing them away with her hand, as if she was irritated. And even though the gash looked painful, she kept staring into the office as if she didn't feel it. This was about a week ago.

A week?

Not knowing what to make of what the woman told him, he continues to give out flyers after she has left. His entire family has posted flyers and distributed them everywhere, from Seoul Station to Namyong-dong, from restaurants and clothing stores to bookstores and Internet cafés. When the flyers were torn off because the family had posted them in a place they weren't supposed to, they reposted them in the same place. They didn't limit it to the area around Seoul Station, either, but handed out and posted flyers in Namdaemun, Chungnim-dong, and even in Sodaemun. They didn't receive a single phone call from the ad they had placed in the newspaper, but some people did call after seeing the flyers. They received a tip that someone like Mom was at a restaurant and rushed over, but it wasn't her; it was a woman around Mom's age who worked there. Once, a caller said that he had invited Mom into his house, and carefully spelled out his address on the phone; filled with expectation, they ran over there, but the address itself didn't exist. There was even someone who said that he would find Mom for them if they would pay him the five-million-won reward up front. But even these calls became sparse after about two weeks. The members of his family, who had rushed around with hope-filled hearts, would often find each other sitting at the base of the Seoul Station clock tower, dejected. When people crumpled the flyer as soon as it was handed to them and threw it on the ground, his younger sister, the writer, picked it up, smoothed it out, and gave it to someone else.

His sister, who came to Seoul Station with an armful of flyers, stands next to him. Her dry eyes glance at his. He relays the woman's words and asks, "Should we go to the Yongsan 2-dong office and look around?" His sister asks, "Why would Mom go there?" Looking despondent, she says, "We can stop by later," and, addressing the people brushing past them, says loudly, "It's our mom—please take a look at it before throwing it away," and hands out flyers. Nobody recognizes his sister, whose picture is sometimes featured in the daily paper's culture section when she publishes a new book. It must be more effective to combine yelling and giving out flyers, as his sister does. People don't throw away her flyers as soon as they turn around, the way they do with his. There aren't many places Mom might go to, other than his siblings' houses. This is the root of his and his family's agony. If Mom had some places she might head for, they would focus their search there, but because there isn't any such place, they have to comb the whole city. When his sister asked, "Why would Mom go there?" he didn't immediately realize that his first job in this city had been at the Yongsan 2-dong office. Because that was thirty years ago.

The wind has turned cool, but beads of sweat dot his face. He's a few years past fifty, a marketing director for a developer of apartment buildings. Today, Saturday, is not a workday, but if Mom hadn't gone missing he would be at the model house in Songdo. His company is recruiting last-minute buyers for units in a large apartment complex there, which will soon be completed. He's worked day and night to reach 100 percent occupancy. All through the spring, he was in charge of the ad campaign and worked on selecting an ordinary housewife as the model, instead of going for the typical professional. During that time, he never got home before midnight; he was so busy with the construction of the model house and wining and dining journalists. On Sundays, he would often escort the CEO and other executives to golf courses in Sokcho or Hoengsong.

"Hyong-chol! Mom's missing!" His younger brother's urgent voice on a midsummer afternoon created a fissure in his daily life, shattering it as if he'd set foot on thin ice. Even as he heard that Father and Mom had been about to get on the subway heading for his brother's house, but that the car had left with only Father aboard, leaving Mom behind in the station, and that she couldn't be located, it didn't occur to him that this would lead to Mom's disappearance. When his brother said that he'd called the police, Hyong-chol wondered whether he was overreacting. Only after a week passed did he put an ad in the paper and call emergency rooms. Every night, they split up into teams and visited homeless shelters, to no avail. Mom, who had been left behind at Seoul Station, disappeared as if she were a figment of a dream. No trace of her remained. He wanted to ask Father whether she had really come to Seoul. Ten days passed since her disappearance, then two weeks, and when it became almost a month, he and his family fumbled around in confusion, as if they had all injured a part of their brains.

He hands his flyers to his sister. "I'm going to check it out."

"You mean Yongsan?"

"Yeah."

"Do you have a hunch?"

"It's the first place I lived in when I came to Seoul."

He tells his sister to check her cell phone often, that he will call her if he discovers anything. These are unnecessary words at this point. His sister, who never used to answer her phone, now picks up before the third ring. He walks toward the line of taxis. Mom worried about his sister Chi-hon, who is in her mid-thirties but is still unmarried. Sometimes Mom called him in the early morning and fretted, "Hyong-chol! Go over to Chi-hon's; she's not answering the phone. She's not answering, and she's not calling me, either—I haven't heard her voice in a month." When he told Mom that Chi-hon would be holed up at home, writing, or that she must have gone somewhere, Mom insisted that he go over to his sister's apartment: "She's alone. She could be sick in bed, or she might have fallen in the bathroom and can't get up. . . ." When he listened to the string of mishaps that might occur to someone living alone, he would be swayed into thinking that any of those things could really happen. Before work or during lunch, he would stop by his sister's apartment at Mom's urging and see a heap of newspapers at her door, signaling Chi-hon's absence. He would gather the newspapers and shove them into a garbage can. When he didn't see any papers or milk delivered at her door, he would keep pressing the doorbell, knowing that she was inside, and she would poke her unkempt face out and grumble, "What now?" Once, when he was ringing her doorbell, a man arrived, seemingly to visit Chi-hon. The man even said hello to him, awkwardly. Before Hyong-chol could ask who he was, the man said, "You look so much like Chi-hon that I don't even need to ask who you are." The man said he'd come by because he had suddenly stopped hearing from her. When Hyong-chol told Mom that his sister seemed to have gone on a trip, or that she was at home and she was fine, Mom would sigh and say, "We won't know about it even if she dies." Then she would ask, "What is it exactly that she does?" His sister wrote novels, and to do this she would disappear for fifteen days or sometimes even a month. When he asked her, "Do you have to do that when you write?" she would mumble, "Next time I'll call Mom." That was it. Even though Mom was like that, the chasm between the family and his sister continued. Mom stopped asking him to go check on Chi-hon after he ignored her requests a few times. She only mentioned once, "I guess you don't have time to listen to me." Because his sister's abrupt silences continued, he figured someone else in the family must be doing Mom's bidding. After Mom went missing, his sister muttered to him, "Maybe I'm being punished. . . ."

There is a lot of traffic between Seoul Station and Sook-myung Women's University. He looks out the car window at the towering gray buildings. He carefully inspects people walking by. In case Mom is in the crowd somewhere.

"Sir, you said the Yongsan 2-dong office, right?" the taxi driver asks him, turning in front of the university toward Yongsan High School, but Hyong-chol doesn't register the question.

"Sir?"

"Yes?"

"You said the Yongsan 2-dong office, right?"

"Yes."

He walked this street every day when he was twenty but the scenery outside the car window is foreign to him. He wonders if this is the right way. It would actually be more jarring if the district hadn't changed at all in thirty years.

"Since it's Saturday, the office is probably closed."

"I guess that's right."

The taxi driver is about to say something else, but Hyong-chol takes out a flyer from his pocket and pushes it toward him. "If you see someone like this while you're driving around, please let me know."

The driver glances at the flyer. "Is this your mother?"

"Yes."

"How terrible . . ."

Last fall, he didn't do anything even though his sister called to say that Mom was acting strangely. He thought that, at her age, Mom would have ailments and illnesses. His sister ruefully told him that Mom seemed to be fainting from her headaches, but when he called home Mom answered warmly, "Hyong-chol!" When he asked, "Is anything going on?" Mom laughed and said, "I wish there was something going on! Don't worry about us. What would be going on with two old folks like us? Take care of yourselves."

"Come visit us in Seoul."

Mom said, "Okay, we will," and trailed off. His sister, angry at his indifference, came to his office and shoved into his hands a scan of Mom's brain. His sister related the doctor's words that a stroke had occurred in Mom's brain without her realization. When he listened placidly, she said, "Hyong-chol! Are you really Yun Hyong-chol?" and stared into his eyes.

"She said nothing was going on, so what's all this?"

"You trust her? Mom always says that. That's Mom's mantra. You know it's true. You know she's just saying that because she feels guilty about being a burden to you."

"Why does she feel guilty?"

"How would I know? Why do you make her feel guilty?"

"What did I do?"

"Mom's been saying that for a long time. You know she has. Let me ask you, why in the world does Mom feel guilty when it comes to you?"

———

Thirty years ago, after he passed the fifth-level civil-service exam, the first placement he received was at the Yong-san 2-dong office. In high school, when he didn't get into any university in Seoul, Mom couldn't believe it. For her it was an obvious reaction. From the early days of elementary school through high school, he had always been the best student in his class. Until he failed to get into college, he had always placed first, no matter which test he took. When he was in sixth grade, he got the best score in the middle-school entrance exam, which allowed him to attend school tuition-free. For three straight years, he was the best student at school, so he never had to pay a cent. He was admitted to high school as the first in his class. "I wish I could pay my Hyong-chol's tuition at least once," Mom would exclaim in pride. It was hard for her to understand how someone who was the top student throughout high school didn't pass the college entrance exam. When they heard that he not only failed to pass at the top but didn't make it at all, Mom was puzzled. "If you can't pass, who can?" she asked herself. He had been planning to study hard in college to remain at the top of his class. It wasn't really a plan—it was his only option. The only way he could go to college was on scholarship. But because he didn't pass, he had to find another path. He didn't have the luxury even to consider retaking the test the following year, and he soon figured out what to do: he took two civil-service exams and passed both. He left home, taking the first assignment he received. And a few months later, he learned that there was a night law college in Seoul and decided to apply for it. He realized that he needed his high-school graduation certificate. If he sent a letter asking for a copy and waited for it to come by mail from the countryside, it would arrive after the application was due. So he wrote a letter to his father, requesting that he go to the bus terminal with a copy of the certificate and ask someone coming to Seoul to take it for him. He asked his father to call him at work after doing that—if his father could tell him what time the bus was due to arrive, he would go to the terminal and get the certificate from the person carrying it. He waited and waited, but there was no phone call. In the middle of the night, as he was wondering what he could do about the application, which was due the next day, someone banged on the door of the office, where he was living at the time. The employees had to take turns for night duty, but since he didn't have a place to stay, it was decided that he would live in the night duty room: he was on duty every night. The banging went on as if it would break down the door; when he went out, a young man stood in the darkness.

"Is this your mother?"

His mom was standing behind the young man, shivering in the cold. Before he could say anything she said, "Hyong-chol! It's me! Mom!" The young man looked at his watch and said, "There's only seven minutes until the curfew!" and, turning to Hyong-chol's mom, said "Goodbye!" and ran into the darkness to beat the government-imposed deadline.

Father had been away from home. When Hyong-chol's sister read Mom his letter, Mom fretted, then went to his high school and got a copy of his graduation certificate and hopped on the train. It was the first time in her life that she'd ridden a train. That young man had seen Mom at Seoul Station asking people how to get to Yongsan-dong. Hearing her say that there was something she absolutely had to get to her son that night, he was compelled to bring her to the office himself. Hyong-chol's mom was wearing blue plastic sandals in the middle of winter. During fall harvest, she had hurt her foot, near her big toe, with a scythe, and because it hadn't fully healed, the plastic sandals were the only shoes she could wear. His mom left her sandals outside the night duty room before entering. "I don't know if it's too late!" she said, and took out his graduation certificate. Mom's hands were frozen. Grasping them, he vowed to himself that he would make these hands and this woman happy, no matter what. But a rebuke tumbled out of his mouth, asking her how she could follow a stranger just because he told her to. Mom scolded him right back: "How can you live without trusting people? There are more people who are good than people who are bad!" And she smiled her typical optimistic smile.

———

He stands in front of the closed office and studies the building. Mom couldn't have come here. If she could figure out how to get here, she could have gone to one of her children's places. The woman who said she had seen his mom here remembered her because of her eyes. She said his mom was wearing blue plastic sandals. Blue plastic sandals. He remembers just now that the shoes Mom had on when she went missing were low-heeled beige sandals. Father had told him. But the woman who had told him that Mom's sandals had cut into her foot because she had walked so far had definitely said that they were blue. He peers into the office, then looks around the streets leading to Posong Girls' High School and Eunsong Church.

Does the night duty room still exist in that office?

That night duty room was where he slept next to Mom all those years ago, sharing a blanket. Next to the woman who had boarded the Seoul-bound train without a plan, to bring a graduation certificate to her son. That must have been the last time he had lain next to Mom like that. A chilly draft seeped in, in waves from the wall facing the street. "I can fall asleep better if I'm next to the wall," Mom said, and switched sides with him. "It's drafty," he said, and got up to stack his bag and books next to the wall, to block out the wind. He piled the clothes he had been wearing that day next to the wall, too. "It's fine," Mom said, pulling him by the hand. "Go to bed; you have to get up for work tomorrow."

"How's your first taste of Seoul?" he asked, looking up at the ceiling, lying next to his mom.

"Nothing special," Mom said, and laughed. She turned to look at him, and started to talk of times gone by. "You're my first child. This isn't the only thing that you got me to do for the first time. Everything you do is a new world for me. You got me to do everything for the first time. You were the first who made my belly swollen, and the first to breastfeed. I was your age when I had you. When I saw your red, sweaty face, eyes shut, for the first time . . . People say that when they have their first child they're surprised and happy, but I think I was sad. Did I really have this baby? What do I do now? I was so afraid that at first I couldn't even touch your squirmy little fingers. You were holding those tiny hands in such tight fists. If I opened your fists up one finger at a time, you smiled. They were so small that I thought, If I keep touching them they might disappear. Because I didn't know anything. I got married at seventeen, and when I didn't get pregnant until I was nineteen, Aunt kept saying I probably wouldn't be able to have children, so when I found out I was pregnant with you, the first thing I thought was, Now I don't have to hear that from her—that was what made me the most excited. Later, I was happy to see your fingers and toes grow every day. When I was tired, I went over to you and opened your fingers. Touched your toes. When I did that, I felt energized. When I first put shoes on you, I was really excited. When you toddled over to me, I laughed so much; even if someone had spilled out a heap of gold and silver and jewels in front of me, I wouldn't have laughed like that. And how do you think I felt when I sent you to school? When I pinned your name tag and a handkerchief on your chest, I felt so grown up. How can I compare the happiness I got watching your legs get thicker with anything else? Every day, I sang, Grow and grow, my baby. And then, one day, you were bigger than me."

He gazed at Mom as the words spilled out like a confession. She rolled over onto her side to face him and stroked his hair. "Even though I said, 'I hope you grow tall and big,' when you got bigger than me I was scared, even though you were my child."

He cleared his throat and turned to stare at the ceiling again, to hide his watery eyes.

"Unlike other children, you didn't need me to tell you anything. You did everything by yourself. You are handsome, and you were good in school. I'm so proud, and sometimes I'm amazed that you came from me. . . . If it weren't for you, when would I have the chance to come to Seoul?"

He resolved then that he would earn a lot of money so that when Mom came back to this city she would be able to sleep in a warm place. That he wouldn't allow her to sleep in the cold again. Some time passed. In a low voice, Mom said, "Hyong-chol." He heard her voice from far away, half asleep. Mom reached out and stroked his head. She sat up and looked over his sleeping figure and touched his forehead. "I'm sorry." Mom quickly took her hand away to wipe her tears, but they dropped on his face.

When he woke up at dawn, his mom was sweeping the floor of the office. He tried to stop her, but Mom said, "I might as well, I'm not doing anything," and, as if she would be punished if she weren't doing anything, washed the floor with a wet mop and thoroughly cleaned the employees' desks. Mom's breath was visible, and the top of her swollen foot was pushing against her blue sandal. As they waited for the nearby bean-sprout-soup place to open so they could eat breakfast, Mom's hands made the office gleam.

———

This house is still here. His eyes grow wide. He has been poking around the narrow alleys filled with parked cars, looking for Mom. Now, as the sun hangs low in the sky, he finds himself in front of the house where he rented a room thirty years ago. He reaches out to touch the gate, amazed. The sharp arrowlike steel spikes on top of the gate are still there, the same as thirty years ago. The woman who once loved him but ended up leaving him would sometimes hang a plastic bag filled with Chinese buns on the gate when he wasn't there. All the other houses nearby have been converted to townhouses or studio apartments.

He reads the ad posted on the gate:

———

100,000 WON PER MONTH,
WITH A DEPOSIT OF 10 MILLION WON.
150,000 WON PER MONTH POSSIBLE
WITH A DEPOSIT OF 5 MILLION WON.

8 pyong, standard sink, shower in bathroom.
Close to Namsan, good for exercising.
Can get to Kangnam in 20 minutes, Chongno in 10 minutes.

Cons: Small bathroom. You're not going to live in it.
It's probably hard to find something this cheap in Yongsan.
The reason I'm moving: I got a car and need a parking
space. Please text or e-mail. I'm renting the room
myself to save on broker fees.

Having read even the cell-phone number and the e-mail
address, he pushes the gate slowly. The gate opens, just as it
did thirty years ago. He looks inside. A U-shaped house, the
same as thirty years ago, the door to each unit facing the courtyard. The door of the unit he used to live in has a padlock on it.

"Anyone home?" he calls out, and two or three doors
open.

Two young women with short hair and two boys around
seventeen look at him. He steps into the courtyard.

"Have you seen this person?" He shows the flyer to the
young women first, then quickly hands one to the boys, who
are about to shut their door. There are two girls around the
same age peering out from inside the boys' room. The boys,
thinking he's looking into their room, bang the door shut. The
outside looks the same as thirty years ago, but each unit has
become a studio. The owners must have renovated, creating
one space, combining the kitchen and the room. He can see a
sink in the corner of the women's unit.

"No," the young women say, and hand him the flyer.
They have sleep in their eyes; perhaps they were napping.
They watch him turn around and head back to the gate. He's
about to step outside when the boys' door opens and someone

calls, "Wait! I think this grandmother was sitting in front of the gate a few days ago."

When he approaches the room, the other boy sticks his head out and says, "No, I told you this isn't her. This lady is young. That lady was really wrinkly. Her hair wasn't like this, either—she was a beggar."

"But her eyes were the same. Look only at her eyes; they were just like these. If we find her, are you really going to give us five million won?"

"I'll give you some money as long as you tell me exactly what happened, even if you don't find her." He asks the boys to step outside. The young women, who had closed their door, open it again and look out.

"That lady was the one from the bar down the street. They keep her locked up because she has dementia, and it looked like she snuck out and got lost. The owner of the bar came and took her home."

"Not that lady; I saw this lady, too. She'd hurt her foot. It was covered in pus. She kept chasing away flies . . . though I didn't look closely, because she smelled and was dirty."

"And? Did you see where she went?" Hyong-chol asks the boy.

"No. I just went in. She kept trying to come in, so I slammed the gate. . . ."

Nobody else had seen Mom. The boy follows him out, saying, "I really did see her!" He looks down the alleys, running ahead of Hyong-chol. Hyong-chol gives the boy a hundred-thousand-won check as he leaves. The boy's eyes sparkle. Hyong-chol asks the boy to get the lady to stay with him if he

sees her again and to give him a call. Not listening very carefully, the boy says, "Then you'll give me five million won?"
Hyong-chol nods. The boy asks for a few more flyers. He says
he will hang them up at the gas station where he works part-
time. He says that if Hyong-chol finds his mom from that he
should be rewarded with five million won, because it will be
thanks to him. Hyong-chol tells him he will.

They have faded—promises he made to himself for Mom,
who changed places with him in the night duty room to protect him from the draft, saying, "I can fall asleep better if I'm
next to the wall." The pledge he had made that Mom would
sleep in a warm room when she came back to this city.

He takes a cigarette from his pocket and puts it in his
mouth. He doesn't know exactly when it happened, but at
some point his emotions ceased to belong only to him. He
went about his life, having mostly forgotten about Mom.
*What was I doing when Mom was left behind on that unfamiliar
subway-station platform, having failed to get on the train with Father?*
He looks up once more at the office and turns back. *What was I
doing?* He hangs his head. The day before Mom went missing,
he went out drinking with his co-workers, but it didn't end
well. His co-worker Kim, who was usually respectful and
polite, made a subtle dig at him after a few drinks, pronounc-
ing him "clever." At work, Hyong-chol was in charge of the
sale of the apartments near Songdo, in Inchon, and Kim over-
saw the sale of the apartments near Yongin. Kim's remark
referred to Hyong-chol's idea of giving out concert tickets as

promotional gifts for people coming to the model home. This wasn't his idea but that of his sister, the writer. When Chi-hon was over at his house, his wife gave her a bath mat that had been the promotional gift for the last apartment sale, and his sister said, "I don't know why companies think homemakers like this kind of thing."

He had been wondering what to give as a promotional gift this time, so he asked, "Well, what do you think would be memorable?"

"I'm not sure, but people quickly forget about things like this. Wouldn't it be better if it were a fountain pen or something? Think about it. Do you think your wife would be happy if you got her kitchen gadgets for her birthday? If you get a mat to promote an apartment sale, you'd just forget about it. But I think I would be pleasantly surprised if it was a book or a movie ticket, and I'd probably remember it. If I had to make plans to use it, I'd keep remembering how I got it. Am I the only one who thinks like that?" His sister left the mat behind when she went home.

At a meeting the following week, someone mentioned promotional gifts. Everyone liked his suggestion of a cultural gift. A singer with many middle-aged fans was performing, in a convenient coincidence, a long-running concert series, so Hyong-chol got a block of tickets. He was praised by his boss; perhaps it was a singer his boss liked. A survey showed that the concert tickets heightened the company's image. Though this probably had nothing to do with the promotional gifts, his apartments in Songdo had almost all sold, whereas the occupancy rate of Kim's Yongin apartments stood at only 60 percent. So, when Kim made the remark, Hyong-chol just laughed it off, saying it was dumb luck, but after a few more drinks, Kim commented that if Hyong-chol used his clever brain somewhere else he could have become the head prosecutor. Kim knew that Hyong-chol had gone to a law college and had studied for the bar exam. He went on to comment that he didn't know what scheme Hyong-chol had used to get promoted so quickly when he wasn't even a graduate of Yonsei University or Koryo University, which produced the main power players in the company. In the end, Hyong-chol dumped out the liquor that Kim had poured in his glass and left. The next morning, when his wife said she would visit their daughter, Chin, instead of going to Seoul Station, he'd planned to meet his parents himself. Father wanted to stop by his younger son's, who had just moved to a new place. Hyong-chol had meant to pick them up and drop them off at his brother's, but once he was at work he felt a chill coming on and had a headache. Father did say that he could find his way. . . . Instead of going to Seoul Station, Hyong-chol went to a sauna near work. As he sweated in the sauna, which he often visited the day after he drank too much, Father was getting on the train without Mom.

————

As a boy, Hyong-chol made up his mind to become a prosecutor to get Mom to return home. She had left because she was disappointed by Father. One spring day, as flowers bloomed all around the village, Father had brought home a woman with fair skin, who smelled fragrant, like face powder. When the woman came in through the front gate, Mom left through the back. The woman, trying to buy her way into Hyong-chol's cold heart, topped his lunch every day with a fried egg. He would storm out of the house with his lunch container, which the woman had wrapped carefully in a scarf, and he'd leave it on top of the large condiment jars in the back yard and go to school. His siblings, watching him always, if surreptitiously, took the lunches the woman made. One misty morning, on the way to school, he gathered his siblings at the creek snaking by the cemetery. He dug a hole near a bloom- ing weeping willow and made them bury their lunches. His brother tried to run away with his lunch, but Hyong-chol caught him and hit him. His sisters obediently buried their lunches. He thought the woman would no longer be able to make them lunch. But the woman went to town and bought new containers. They weren't yellowish aluminum containers but special ones that kept the rice warm. Awed, his siblings touched the new containers cautiously. When the woman handed them their lunches, his brother and sisters looked at him. He would push his lunch toward the end of the porch and leave for school alone. His siblings would wait until he was out of sight, then go to school themselves, carrying their warm lunches in their hands. Perhaps having heard from someone that he wasn't taking the lunches made by the woman and that he wasn't eating, either, Mom came to school to find him. It was about ten days after the woman had come to live with them.

"Mom!" Tears spilled from his eyes.

Mom led him to the hill behind the school. She pulled up the legs of his pants to reveal his smooth calves, grabbed a switch, and hit them.

"Why aren't you eating? Did you think I would be happy if you didn't eat?"

Mom's thrashing was harsh. He had been upset that his siblings weren't listening to him, and now he couldn't understand why Mom was whipping him. His heart brimmed with resentment. He didn't know why she was so angry.

"Are you going to take your lunch? Are you?"

"No!"

"You little . . ."

Mom's whipping became swifter. He didn't admit it hurt, not once, and soon Mom grew tired. Instead of running away, he stood still, silent, and suffered her blows.

"Even now?"

The redness bloomed into blood on his calves.

"Even now!" he yelled.

Finally, Mom tossed the switch away. "God, you brat! Hyong-chol!" she said, embracing him and bursting into sobs. Eventually, she stopped, and tried to persuade him. He had to eat, she said, no matter who cooked the meals; she would be less sad if he ate well. Sadness. It was the first time he'd heard Mom say the word "sad." He didn't know why his eating properly would make Mom less sad. Since Mom had left because of that woman, it seemed to him that she would be sad if he ate the woman's food, but she told him the opposite was true. She would be less sad if he ate, even if it was that woman's food. No, he didn't understand it, but since he didn't want her to be sad, he said, grouchily, "I'll eat it."

"That's my boy." Mom's eyes, filled with tears, lit up along with her smile.

"Then promise you'll come home!" he insisted.

Mom faltered. "I don't want to come home."

"Why? Why?"

"I never want to see your father again."

Tears ran down his cheeks. Mom acted as if she would really never come home. Maybe that was why she'd said he had to eat, no matter who cooked the food. He got scared.

"Mom, I'll do everything. I'll work in the fields and the paddies and sweep the yard and bring the water. I'll grind the rice and make the fire. I'll chase the mice and I'll kill the chicken for the ancestral rites. Just come back!"

For ancestral rites or holidays, Mom always begged Father or any other male in the house to kill a chicken for her. Mom, who went into the fields after a heavy rain and propped up fallen beanstalks all day, who practically carried Father on her back to bring him home when he was drunk, who beat the pig's behind with a stick when it escaped from the pen to usher it back inside, couldn't kill a chicken. When Hyong-chol caught a fish from the creek, she wouldn't touch it until it was dead. When every student was instructed to bring in the tail of a mouse to show that everyone had captured a mouse at home on mouse-catching days, other children's moms caught a mouse and cut off the tail and wrapped it up in paper to take to school. But Mom shrank away even from hearing about it. A woman of sturdy build, she couldn't bring herself to catch a mouse. If she went to the shed to get some rice and encountered a mouse, she would scream and run outside. Aunt would glare disapprovingly and cluck at Mom when she rushed out of the shed, red-faced. But even though he promised he would kill chickens and chase mice, Mom didn't say she would come home.

"I'll become an important person," Hyong-chol promised.

"What are you going to be?"

"A prosecutor!"

Mom's eyes sparkled then. "If you want to be a prosecutor, you have to study hard. A lot more than you think you do. I know someone who wanted be a prosecutor and studied night and day and never made it and went crazy."

"I'll do it if you come home. . . ."

Mom looked into his anxious eyes. She smiled. "Yes. You can do it. You were able to say Ma before you were a hundred days old. Even though no one taught you to read, you learned to read as soon as you went to school, and you're ranked first in your class." She sighed. "Why would I leave that house when you're there—why didn't I think of that? You're there."

Mom stared at his calves speckled with blood, then turned around and squatted, telling him to climb on her back. He looked at her. Mom turned her head. "Get on," she said. "Let's go home."

That was how, in the late afternoon, Mom came home that day. She shoved that woman out of the kitchen and cooked. And when the woman and Father went to live in another house in town, Mom rolled up her sleeves, ran over to their house, grabbed the rice pot hanging over their hearth, and sent it rushing down the creek. It seemed as if Mom became a fighter so that she could keep the promise she had made to Hyong-chol, and return home. When Father and the woman, unable to stand Mom's harassment, left the town altogether, Mom called Hyong-chol to her and sat him down before her, knee to knee. Calmly, she asked Hyong-chol, who was once again frightened that she might leave as well, "How much studying did you do today?" When he pulled out the test he had gotten a perfect score on, Mom's gloomy eyes regained their fire. She looked at the test, on which his teacher had circled in red every correct answer, and grabbed him in a hug.

"Oh, my baby!"

Mom pampered him while Father was gone. She let him ride Father's bicycle. She gave him Father's sleeping mat and covered him with Father's blanket. She scooped rice for him into the big rice bowl, which only Father had used. She placed the first bowl of soup in front of him. When his siblings started to eat, she would scold, "Your brother hasn't even picked up his spoon!" When the fruit vendor came by with a rubber bin filled with grapes, she traded a half bowl of sesame seeds drying in the yard for some grapes and saved them for him, telling the other children, "This here is for your brother." And every time she did that, Mom reminded him, "You have to become a prosecutor."

He thought he had to become a prosecutor to keep Mom at home.

. . .

That fall, Mom harvested rice and hulled it and dried it by herself, without Father. At dawn, she went to the fields and, bent over, cut rice stalks with her scythe, stripped the grain, and spread it on the ground in the sun to dry. She came home when it got dark. When Hyong-chol tried to help, Mom said, "You go study," and pushed him toward his desk. On warm Sundays after all the rice was harvested, Mom would take his siblings to the field in the hills to dig for sweet potatoes, but she would nudge him toward his desk. They would come back near dusk pushing a wheelbarrow filled with russet sweet potatoes. His brother, who had wanted to stay home to study but had been forced to go with Mom, hunched over the well, scrubbing the dirt from under his fingernails.

"Mom! Is Hyong-chol that important?"

"Yes! He's that important!" Mom rapped his brother on the head without giving the question a second thought.

"Then you don't need us?" His brother's cheeks were flushed from the crisp air.

"No! I don't need you."

"Then we're going to go live with Father!"

"What?" Mom was about to give his brother another rap on the head but stopped. "You're important, too. You are all important! Come here, my important children!" Everyone laughed. Sitting in the glow of the room in front of his desk, listening to his family at the well outside, Hyong-chol smiled, too.

. . .

It's not clear exactly when, but Mom stopped locking the gate at night. Soon after, when she scooped rice for everyone in the morning, she started to put some in Father's rice bowl and leave it under a blanket in the warmest part of the room. Hyong-chol studied even harder while Father was gone. Mom continued to refuse to let him help in the fields. Even when she was yelling at her other children that they had left the peppers spread out in the yard in the rain, she lowered her voice if she thought he was studying. In those days, Mom's face was always crumpled with fatigue and worry, but when he studied by reading out loud, the flesh around her eyes became brighter, as if she had dabbed on powder. Mom opened and closed the door to his room quietly. She silently slid a plate of boiled sweet potatoes or persimmons into the room, then gently closed the door. One winter night when the snow drifted onto the porch, Father walked in the open gate, cleared his throat, took his shoes and smacked them against the wall to get the snow off, and opened the door. It was so cold that everyone was sleeping together. Through half-open eyes, Hyong-chol watched Father touch everyone's head and gaze down at them all. He saw Mom placing on the table the rice bowl she'd kept in the warmest part of the room, saw her bringing sheets of seaweed toasted with perilla oil and putting them next to the rice bowl, and watched as she placed a bowl of rice-boiled water next to the rice bowl without a word—as if Father had left that morning and had come back at night, instead of having left in the summer and returned sheepishly in the bitter cold of winter.

· · ·

When Hyong-chol graduated from college and passed the entrance exam for the company he works at now, Mom wasn't happy. She didn't even smile when the neighbors congratulated her on Hyong-chol's employment at a top corporation. When he came home with the traditional gift of underwear bought with his first paycheck, she barely looked at it, and coldly shot at him, "What about what you were going to be?"

He replied simply that he would work hard at the company, save for two years, and start studying again.

——

Now he reflects on this. When she was younger, Mom was a presence that got him to continue building his resolve as a man, as a human being.

——

It was when Mom brought his sister, who had just graduated from middle school, to the city to stay with him that she started to tell him she was sorry all the time. She brought his sister from the country when he was twenty-four. It was before he was able to save money, before he could take the bar exam again. She kept her eyes lowered.

"Since she's a girl, she has to get more schooling. Somehow you have to make it possible for her to go to school here. I can't have her live like me."

They met in front of the clock tower at Seoul Station. Before she went home, she suggested a meal of rice and soup. Mom kept picking out the beef in her soup and placing it in his bowl. Even though he said he couldn't eat it all and that she should eat some, Mom kept transferring the meat from her bowl to his. And although it had been her idea to eat, not a single morsel reached her lips.

"Aren't you hungry?" he asked.

"I'm eating, I am," she said, but kept plopping the meat into his bowl. "But you . . . what are you going to do?" Mom put down her spoon, which was rimmed with soup. "It's all my fault. I'm sorry, Hyong-chol."

As she stood in Seoul Station to board the train home, her rough hands with her short-clipped nails buried deep in her pockets, Mom's eyes were ringed with tears. He thought then that her eyes looked like those of a cow, guileless and kind.

———

He calls his sister, who's still at Seoul Station. The day is fading. His sister stays silent when she hears his voice. It seems that she wants him to speak first. They listed everyone's cell-phone numbers on the flyer, but his sister has gotten most of the calls. Most of them were false reports. One guy said, "The lady is with me right now." He even gave a detailed explanation of where he was. His sister rushed by taxi to the footbridge the caller directed her to, and found a young drunk, a man, not even a woman, snoring away, so inebriated that he wouldn't have noticed if someone had carted him away.

"She isn't here," he tells his sister.

His sister releases the breath she was holding.

"Are you going to stay at the station?" he asks.

"For a little while . . . I still have some flyers."

"I'll come to you. Let's get some dinner."

"I'm not hungry."

"Then we'll have a drink."

"A drink?" she asks, and falls silent for a moment. "I got a phone call," she says, "from a pharmacist at Sobu Pharmacy, in front of Sobu Market, in Yokchon-dong. He said he'd seen a flyer his son had brought home. He thought he saw someone like Mom in Yokchon-dong two days ago . . . but he said that she was wearing blue plastic sandals. That she must have walked so much that the top of her foot had a gash, and that it was infected all the way to her toenails, and that he put some medicine on it. . . ."

Blue sandals? His cell phone slides off his ear.

"Brother!"

He presses the phone back to his ear.

"I'm going to go over there. Do you want to come?"

"Yokchon-dong?" he asks. "Do you mean that Sobu Market we used to live near?"

"Yeah."

"Okay."

· · ·

He doesn't want to go home. He doesn't have anything particular to say when he meets his sister. When he called her, he was thinking only, I don't want to go home. But Yokchon-dong? He raises his hand to flag a taxi. He doesn't understand. Several people have called to say they saw someone like Mom wearing blue plastic sandals. Strangely, they all said they'd seen her in a neighborhood he's lived in. Kaebong-dong, Taerim-dong, Oksu-dong, under the Naksan Apartments in Tongsung-dong, Suyu-dong, Singil-dong, Chongnung. If he stopped by, the callers would say they saw her three days ago, or some-times a week ago. Someone even said he'd seen her a month before she went missing. Every time he received a tip, he went to that neighborhood, alone or with his siblings or with Father. Even though they all said they'd seen her, he couldn't find anyone like Mom wearing blue plastic sandals. After hear-ing their stories, he could only post some flyers on the utility poles in the neighborhood, or on a tree in the park, or inside a telephone booth, just in case. When he passed the places he used to live, he would pause and peek in at these spaces where others were now living.

No matter where he lived, Mom never came by herself to his house. A family member always went to greet Mom at Seoul Station or the Express Bus Terminal. And once in Seoul, Mom didn't go anywhere until someone came to take her to her next destination. When she went to his brother's, he came to get her; when she went to his sister's, she came to get her. Nobody ever said it out loud, but at some moment he and his family tacitly came to believe Mom couldn't go anywhere in this city by herself. So, whenever Mom came to Seoul, someone was always with her. He realized, after placing the newspaper ad for Mom and passing out flyers, that he had lived in twelve different neighborhoods. Now he straightens and looks up. Yokchon-dong, he remembers, was the first place where he was able to buy a house.

"It's Full Moon Harvest in a few days. . . ." In the taxi heading for Yokchon-dong, his sister nervously rubs her fingernails with her hand. He's thinking the same thing. He clears his throat and frowns. The Full Moon Harvest holiday is several days long. The media reports every time that this year more people were going abroad during the holiday than ever before. Until a couple of years ago, people criticized those who went abroad during the holiday, but now people blatantly say, "Ancestors, I'll be back," and go to the airport. When people started to hold ancestral rites in time-share vacation condos, they worried whether the ancestral spirits would be able to find them, but now people just hop on planes. This morning, his wife, who was reading the paper, said, as if it were news, "It says right here that more than a million people will be going abroad this year."

"People sure have a lot of money," he replied, at which she mumbled, "People who can't leave—well, they're not too smart."

Father just watched them.

His wife continued, "Since their friends go abroad during the Full Moon Harvest, the kids were saying, I wish we could do that, too." When he glared at his wife, unable to listen to it any longer, she explained, "You know how kids are sensitive to that kind of thing." Father got up from the table and went into his room.

"Are you crazy? Is this something to talk about right now?" he snapped, and his wife retorted, "Look, I said the kids said that; did I say I wanted to? Can't I even relay what the kids said? It's so frustrating. I'm supposed to live without saying anything?" She got up and left the table.

"Shouldn't we hold the ancestral rites?" Chi-hon asks.

"Since when did you think about the ancestral rites? You never even came home for the holidays, and now you care about Full Moon Harvest?"

"I was wrong. I shouldn't have been that way."

He watches his sister as she stops rubbing her fingernails and sticks her hands in her jacket pockets. She still hasn't gotten rid of that habit.

———

When they lived together in Seoul, when he had to sleep in the same room as his brother and his sister, his sister took her place nearest the wall, he lay in the middle, and his brother lay near the other wall. Just about every night, he'd be smacked in the head and wake up to find his brother's hand draped across his face. He would take it off carefully and be about to fall asleep again when his sister's hand would be flung onto his chest. It was the way they used to sleep in the large room at home, rolling around as much as they pleased. One night, he let out a yell when he got punched in the eye. His siblings woke up.

"Hey! You!"

His sister, belatedly figuring out what had happened, hurriedly stuck her hands in the pockets of the cotton pants she wore to bed and fidgeted nervously.

"If you're going to keep this up, just go home!"

When morning came, his sister really went home to Mom, taking all of her things. Mom brought her back to Seoul right away, telling her to get on her knees before him and ask for his forgiveness. His sister, obstinate, didn't move.

"Ask him to forgive you!" Mom said, but his sister didn't budge.

His sister was gentle, but if she had her mind set on something, nobody could move her. Once, when he was in middle school, he had forced his sister to wash his sneakers against her will. Usually she obediently washed them clean, but that day she got upset and took them, his new but grubby sneakers, to the creek and sent them downstream. He ran all the way along the creek to retrieve his floating shoes. Later, it became a cherished memory that only siblings could share, but at the time, he came home angry with only one sneaker, which had turned green from the slimy water and clinging algae, and told on his sister. Even when Mom picked up the poker, asking where his sister had learned to be so ill-tempered, she wouldn't say she was sorry. Instead, she got angry at Mom. "I said I didn't want to! I told him I didn't want to! And from now on I'm not going to do anything I don't want to do!"

In their small room, Mom ordered his obstinate sister: "I told you to ask him to forgive you. I told you your brother was your parent here. If you don't correct your habit of taking your things and leaving because your brother scolded you, this will stay with you your entire life. If something doesn't go your way when you are married, are you going to take your things and leave even then?"

The more Mom told her to ask for his forgiveness, the deeper his sister's hands burrowed into her pockets. Saddened, Mom sighed. "Now this child won't listen to me. This child is ignoring me because I don't have anything and have no education." Only when Mom's lament turned into teardrops did his sister say, "That's not it, Mom!" To stop Mom from continuing to cry, she had to say, "I'll ask for forgiveness, I'll say I'm sorry," and she took her hands out of her pockets and asked him to forgive her. From then on, his sister slept with her hands in her pockets. And any time he raised his voice, she'd quickly stuff them there.

After Mom went missing, when someone pointed something out, even something trivial, his stubborn sister would admit, subdued, "I was wrong, I shouldn't have done that."

———

"Who's going to wash the windows at home?" Chi-hon asks him.

"What are you talking about?"

"If we called around this time of year, Mom was always cleaning the windows."

"The windows?"

"Yes, of course. She'd always say, 'How can we have dirty windows when the family will be coming for Full Moon Harvest?'"

The many windows of their country home flash before his eyes. The house, newly rebuilt a few years ago, has windows in every room, especially in the living room, unlike the old house, which had one sole windowpane in the door.

"When I suggested that she hire someone to clean the windows, she said, 'Who's going to come to this country hole to do that?'" His sister heaves a sigh and stretches her hand to the taxi window and rubs it.

"When we were little, she took off all the doors in the house around this time of year—remember?" she asks.

"I do."

"Do you remember?"

"I said I do!"

"Liar."

"Why do you think I'm lying? I remember. She used to paste maple leaves on the doors. Even though Aunt gave her a hard time about it."

"So you really do remember. Remember going to Aunt's to pick maple leaves?"

"I remember."

———

Before the new house was built, Mom would choose a sunny day around Full Moon Harvest and take off every single door in the house. She would scrub the doors with water and dry them in the sun and make some paste and brush new, half-translucent mulberry paper onto the doors. Whenever Hyong-chol saw doors taken off their jambs, drying, leaning against the wall of the house, he would think, Ah, it's almost Full Moon Harvest.

Why didn't anyone help Mom brush on the new paper, when there were so many men in the family? His sister probably just fooled around, swirling her finger in the bucket of watery paste. Mom would take the brush and quickly slap the paste on the paper as if she were expertly drawing orchids for a traditional ink painting and, all by herself, would glue the paper on the clean doorframe with sure strokes. Her gestures were lighthearted and cheerful. Mom did work that he wouldn't dare attempt now, even though he's much older than she was at the time, and she did it swiftly and with ease. With a big brush in her hand, she would order his sister, who was playing with the paste, or him, who asked whether he could help, to pick Korean-maple leaves. Even though their yard had a lot of trees, persimmon trees and plum trees and trees of heaven and jujube trees, Mom specifically ordered maple leaves, which they didn't have at home. Once, to get maple leaves, he left the house and passed the alleys and the creek and went all the way down the new road to Aunt's house. As he picked maple leaves there, Aunt asked, "What are you going to do with them? Did your mother tell you to get them? What is this nonsense that your mother's doing? If you look at a door with a maple leaf on it in the winter, you feel colder, but she's going to do it again—even though I'm always telling her to stop!"

When he brought back two handfuls of maple leaves, Mom would neatly place the prettiest ones right next to the handle of every door, one on either side, and paste sheets of mulberry paper over them. The leaves decorated the spot where extra sheets of paper were layered to prevent tearing, right where people touched the door to open and close it. On his door, Mom put three more leaves than on the others, spreading the five leaves like flowers, pressing them carefully with her palms, and asking, "Do you like them?" It looked as if a young child was opening his hand. No matter what Aunt said, they looked beautiful in his eyes. When he said they looked wonderful, a big smile brightened Mom's face. For Mom, who disliked going into the holidays with holey or ripped doors, worn from being flung open and shut throughout summer, pasting on new door paper was the true start of fall and the beginning of Full Moon Harvest. She probably wanted to keep the family from getting colds from the chillier wind after summer, too. Was that, he wondered, the most romance Mom was able to experience in those days?

———

He unconsciously sticks his hands in the pockets of his slacks, like his sister. The maple leaves pasted by the door handles stayed with the family in that house after Full Moon Harvest was over. They stayed through winter and snow; they stayed until new maple leaves sprouted in the spring.

Mom's disappearance was triggering events in his memory, moments, like the maple-leaf doors, he thought he'd forgotten about.

Yokchon-dong isn't the old Yokchon-dong he remembers. When he first bought a house in Seoul, it was a neighborhood of many alleys and houses, but now it's crowded with towering high-rise apartment buildings and clothing stores. He and his sister walk back and forth twice, both in front of and behind the apartment buildings, unable to find Sobu Market, which was in the heart of Yokchon-dong back then. Finally, they ask a passing student where the market is, and it turns out it's in the opposite direction from where they thought it'd be. A big box store has now replaced the telephone booth that he used to walk by every day. He can't find the yarn store where his wife used to take knitting classes, wanting to make sweaters for their newborn daughter.

"I think it's over there, brother!"

Sobu Market, which he remembers as being next to a large road, is buried between new boulevards, and he can't see the signs very well.

"He said it was in front of Sobu Market. . . ." His sister

runs toward the entrance and turns around to look at the stores. "There it is!"

He looks where his sister is pointing and sees the sign that says "Sobu Pharmacy," sandwiched between a snack bar and an Internet café. The bespectacled pharmacist, who is in his mid-fifties, looks up as he and his sister enter. When his sister asks, "You called about the flyer your son had brought you?" the pharmacist takes his glasses off.

"How did your mother happen to go missing?"

This is the most awkward—and frequent—question people have asked since Mom went missing. It's always asked with a mixture of curiosity and judgment. At first they would explain in detail, "Well, you see, she was at the Seoul Station subway . . . ," but now they simply reply, "It just happened," and assume sorrowful expressions. That is the only way they can get past the question.

"Does she have dementia?"

His sister doesn't reply, so he denies it.

"But how can you be like this when you're trying to find her? I called a while ago, and you're only here now?" the pharmacist asks reproachfully, as if they could have been reunited with Mom if they had arrived earlier.

"When did you see her? Does this look like our mom?" His sister pulls out the flyer and points.

The pharmacist says he saw her six days ago. He lives on the third floor of the building, he explains, and he came down at dawn to open the pharmacy's shutters and saw an old woman sleeping by the garbage cans in front of the snack bar next door. He tells them she was wearing blue plastic sandals. He says she'd walked so much that there was a deep cut on her foot, almost to the point of revealing bone. Her wound had become infected and reinfected, so much so that there was almost nothing that could be done.

"As a pharmacist, I couldn't just leave her alone when I saw that gash. I thought at the very least it should be disinfected, so I went inside and brought out some disinfectant and cotton balls, and she woke up. Even though a stranger was touching her foot, she stayed still, completely still—weak. With that kind of cut, it's normal to scream when it's being treated, but she didn't react at all. Surprised me. The infection was so severe, pus kept oozing out. The smell was really awful, too. I don't know how many times I disinfected it. After that I put some ointment on it and a Band-Aid. But it wasn't big enough, so I wrapped her foot with a bandage. It looked like she should be protected somehow, so I went inside to call the police, but then came back out to ask whether she knew anyone. She was eating sushi rolls from the trash. She must have been hungry. I told her I would give her something to eat and she should throw that away, but she didn't, so I grabbed it from her and threw it out. Even though she didn't let go of it when I told her to, she didn't do anything when I took it away. I asked her to come inside the store. She just sat there, as if she didn't understand me. Is she deaf?"

His sister is silent, so he denies it.

"I asked her, 'Where do you live? Do you know someone who can come get you? If you know someone's number, I'll call for you.' But she sat still. Just blinking her eyes. I couldn't do anything, so I went inside and called the police, and when I came out she was gone. It was strange. I was inside for only a few minutes, and she was already gone."

"Our mom wasn't wearing blue plastic sandals," says Chi-hon. "She was wearing beige sandals. Are you sure they were blue plastic ones?"

"Yes. She was wearing a light-blue shirt, and over it a top that was either white or beige, it was so dirty I couldn't tell. Her skirt was something that might've been white once—but that got dirty enough to become beige. It was pleated. Her calves were bloody. They were . . . well, they were ravaged by mosquito bites."

Except for the blue plastic sandals, that's the outfit Mom was wearing when she went missing.

"Mom's wearing a hanbok here. Her hair is completely different. . . . She's really made up in this picture, but she didn't look like this when she went missing. What made you think of our mother when you saw that lady?" His sister seems to hope it wasn't Mom; the woman the pharmacist saw was so pathetic.

"This is the same woman. Her eyes are the same. I herded cows when I was young, so I've seen eyes like hers, earnest and gentle. I recognized her even though she looked different, because those eyes were the same."

His sister collapses into a chair.

"Did the police come?"

"I called them right back, told them they didn't have to come. Like I told you, she was already gone."

He and his sister leave the pharmacy and split up, agreeing to meet at the playground of one of the new apartment complexes in two hours. As the wind picks up, he searches the dimly lit streets around the new apartment buildings that have taken the place of the houses from when he lived here, and his sister looks near Sobu Market, where a few old alleys remain. Because of the pharmacist's story that the woman who might be Mom was eating sushi rolls out of the trash next to the snack bar, he looks carefully at all of the garbage cans near the buildings. He also searches near the recycling bins. He wonders where the house he used to live in could be. It was the second-to-last house in the longest alley in the neighborhood. The alley was so long and dark that when he came home late from work he felt compelled to keep looking behind him before he reached the gate.

His sister is waiting for him on the wooden bench at the playground. She sees his slumped shoulders and slow footsteps and gets up. Because it's late at night, there are no children on the playground, only a handful of old folks sitting around, having come out for a walk.

Did Mom come here to that house?

The first time Mom came to visit here, she got off the train holding a nickel kettle as big as a steamer filled with red-bean porridge. He didn't have a car, and when he took the kettle from her and snapped, "Why did you bring this heavy thing?" Mom just kept smiling. As soon as they turned into the alley, she gestured at a house and asked, "Is this it?" When they walked past it, she pointed at the next house and asked, "Is that it?" She grinned wider when, at last, he stopped in front of his house and announced, "This is it." Mom looked as excited as a young girl on her first journey out of her hometown as she gently pushed the gate open. "Wow, there's a yard, too! A persimmon tree, and—what's this?—grapevines!" As soon as Mom set foot in the house, she poured out a bowl of porridge from the kettle and sprinkled it all around the house. "This is how you ward off bad luck," she said. His wife, who was also a first-time homeowner in the city, opened the door of one of their three rooms and said, excitedly, "This is your room, Mother. When you come to Seoul, you can stay here in comfort." Mom looked inside and exclaimed, with an apologetic expression, "I have my own room!"

That night, past midnight, he heard something in the yard and looked out the window. Mom was walking around. She touched the gate and laid a hand on the grapevine and sat on the steps leading to the front door. She looked up at the night sky and went over to stand under the persimmon tree. He opened the window and called to her, "Come in and sleep."

Mom asked, "Why aren't you sleeping?" and, acting as if she were calling his name for the first time, said, secretively, "Hyong-chol, come out here."

When he reached her, Mom took an envelope from her pocket and put it in his hand. "Now all you need is a nameplate. Use this money to get a nameplate." He looked at Mom, the bulging envelope in his fist. "I'm sorry that I couldn't help you buy this house," she said.

Later, coming back from the bathroom in the early dawn, he opened the door of Mom's room quietly. Mom and

Chi-hon were lying side by side, deep in slumber. Mom seemed to be smiling in her sleep; his sister's arm was, as ever, flung away from her body, freely.

Before that, from her first night with him in the night duty room, there hadn't been a comfortable place for Mom to stay in Seoul. Often he and his siblings went to meet her when she came to Seoul on a chartered bus to attend a relative's wedding. Mom would have a huge load with her. Before the wedding was even over, she would rush him and his siblings to the rented room they were living in. She'd take off the suit she'd worn to the wedding; food wrapped in newspaper or plastic or squash leaves would tumble out of her bundles. It didn't take even a minute for Mom to change into a loose shirt and a pair of floral-print pants, which she'd brought rolled up in a corner of one of her bags. The side dishes that came out of the newspapers and plastic and squash leaves were moved onto plates and into bowls from the cupboard, and Mom brushed off her hands, quickly peeled the covers off the blankets, and washed them. She made kimchi with the salted cabbage she had brought, and scrubbed the pot that had turned black from the coal fire, and cleaned the portable stove until it shone, and sewed the covers back on the blankets after they dried in the sun on the roof, and washed rice and made bean-paste soup and set the table for supper. On the table were generous portions of stewed beef, sautéed anchovies, and sesame-leaf kimchi she'd brought from home. When he and his siblings took a spoonful of rice, Mom placed a piece of stewed beef on each person's spoon. They urged her to eat, but she insisted, "I'm not hungry." After they were done, she cleaned up and filled the rubber basin under the tap with water. She'd go out to buy a watermelon to keep cool in the basin, and then she'd quickly change back into her suit, the only one she had, which she wore only for weddings; then she'd say, "Take me back to the station." It would already be late. "Spend the night and go home tomorrow, Mom," they would say. But she would reply, "I have to go. I have things to do tomorrow." The only thing Mom had to do was work in the rice paddies or the fields; that kind of work could wait until the following day. But Mom always went back on the train that same night. Even though it was really because there was only one room, a small room where her three grown children had to sleep huddled together, unable to move about, Mom just said, "I have to go. I have things to do tomorrow."

He always made renewed resolutions when he brought Mom, exhausted, back to Seoul Station to wait for the night train so she could return home empty-handed. *I'll make money and move to a two-room place. I'll rent a house. I'll buy a house in the city. Then I'll be able to have a room that this woman can sleep in comfortably.* He bought a platform ticket whenever Mom took the night train so he could accompany her to the platform. He would find Mom a seat on the train and hand her a bag full of snacks, maybe banana milk or tangerines.

"Don't fall asleep; remember to get off at Chongup Station."

Mom commanded him—sometimes sadly, sometimes

firmly, "Here in the city, you are your siblings' father and mother."

As he stood there, rubbing his hands together, only twenty-some years old, Mom would get up from her seat and open his hands and straighten his shoulders. "The eldest brother has to be dignified. He has to be the role model. If the eldest brother goes the wrong way, his siblings will go that way, too."

When the train was about to leave, Mom's eyes would fill with tears, and she'd say, "I'm sorry, Hyong-chol."

It would be in the middle of the night when his mom got off at Chongup. The first bus to town would be after six in the morning. His mom would get off the train and walk, in the dark, toward home.

———

"I wish we'd brought more flyers to post around here," he says, burrowing into his jacket against the night chill.

"I'll come back tomorrow and do that," Chi-hon assures him, and she pushes her hands into her pockets.

Tomorrow he has to escort the CEO's aides to the model apartment in Hongchon. He can't afford to excuse himself. "Should I have my wife do it?"

"Let her rest. She's taking care of Father, too."

"Or you can call the youngest."

"Or he'll help me."

"He?"

"Yu-bin. When we find Mom, I'm going to marry him. Mom always wanted me to get married."

"If it's that easy to make up your mind, you should have done it already."

"After Mom went missing, I realized that there's an answer to everything. I could have done everything she wanted me to. It wasn't important. I don't know why I got under her skin over things like that. I'm not going to get on a plane anymore, either."

He pats his sister's shoulder and sighs. Mom didn't like it when his sister got on a plane and went abroad. Mom's opinion was that if it was during war you couldn't help it, but otherwise you couldn't leave your life up to fate like that, as if you didn't care a whit about it. When Mom's meddling about planes got worse, his sister boarded them in secret. Whether it was for business or for pleasure, if she had to take a plane, she left without telling Mom.

"The roses at that house were so beautiful . . . ," his sister says.

He looks at her in the dark. He has just been thinking about those roses. The first spring after he bought his house, Mom visited and suggested they go buy roses. Roses? When the word came out of his mom's mouth he had to ask, "You do mean roses?" as if he'd misheard her.

"Red roses. Why? Isn't there a place that sells them?"

"Yes, there is." He took Mom to a nursery that supplied the saplings lining the streets in Kupabal. "I think this is the prettiest flower," Mom said, and bought many more rosebushes than he had expected. Later that afternoon, she dug holes near the wall around his house and planted them. He had never seen Mom plant something to look at, not to harvest and eat, like beans or potatoes or seedlings of cabbage or radishes or peppers. Watching over her bent form, he asked whether she was planting the roses too close to the wall. Mom looked up at him and said, "That's so that people outside can enjoy them, too." Every spring, the roses came into full blossom. People passing by outside during the rose season paused under the wall and inhaled the scent of roses, just as Mom had hoped. After it rained, red rose petals would be strewn everywhere, having fallen on the other side of the wall.

At the bar in the big box store in Yokchon-dong, his sister, who downed two draft beers in place of dinner, takes out a notebook from her bag, opens it to a particular page, and pushes it toward him. Her face is flushed from drinking on an empty stomach. He tilts the notebook toward the light and reads. Unlike her imaginative and emotional personality, her handwriting is surprisingly compact.

I want to read to children who cannot see.
I want to learn Chinese.
If I earn a lot of money, I want to own a small theater.
I want to go to the South Pole.
I want to go on a pilgrimage to Santiago.

Underneath were thirty more sentences starting with "I."
"What is this?"

"Last New Year's Eve, I wrote down what I wanted to do with my life, other than writing. Just for fun. The things I wanted to do in the next ten years. But I didn't plan on doing anything with Mom. I didn't realize that while I was writing it. But now, when I look at it after Mom's gone missing . . ."

He is drunk. He gets off the elevator and presses the doorbell. No response. He takes his keys out of his pocket and, weaving about, unlocks the door. After he parted with his sister, he went to two more bars. Whenever the image of the woman wearing blue plastic sandals, the woman who could be Mom, the woman who had walked so much that the sandals dug deep into her foot, practically revealing the bones, danced in front of his eyes, he downed another drink.

The light is on in the living room, which is quiet. The statue of Mary that Mom brought watches him. Stumbling, he heads for his bedroom, but pauses to quietly push open the door to his daughter's room, where Father is staying. He can see Father sleeping on his side, on a mat on the floor next to his daughter's bed. He goes inside and pulls up the blanket his father had pushed off in his sleep, and comes back out, gently closing the door behind him. In the kitchen, he pours himself a glass of water from the carafe on the table, and looks around him as he drinks it. Nothing has changed. The hum of the refrigerator is the same, and so is the sink piled with dishes his wife has left undone; she always puts off doing the dishes. He hangs his head, then ventures into his room and looks down at his sleeping wife. A necklace glints at her throat. He grabs the blankets covering her and yanks them off. She sits up, rubbing her eyes.

"When did you get home?" She sighs at his roughness, which contains a silent scolding: How can you sleep! Ever since Mom disappeared, he has started to take things out on everyone. He gets angrier when he comes home. When his brother called to see how the search was going, he answered a few questions but then erupted, "Don't you have anything to tell me? What the hell are you doing?" When Father announced that he would return home because there was nothing he could do here in Seoul, he yelled, "And what are you going to do in the country?" In the morning, Hyong-chol would leave without glancing at the breakfast his wife made him.

"Have you been drinking?" His wife wrests the blankets from his grip and straightens them.

"How can you sleep?" He says it out loud now.

His wife smooths her nightgown.

"I said, how can you sleep!"

"What am I supposed to do, then?" his wife yells back.

"It's your fault!" His voice is slurred. Even he knows that this is a stretch.

"Why is it my fault?"

"You should have gone to meet them!"

"I told you I was going to bring food to Chin."

"Why did you have to go right then? My parents were coming up from the country so we could celebrate their birthdays!"

"Father said he could find his way! And we're not the only family in the city. And they wanted to go to your brother's that day. And your sisters are here, too. Your parents don't always have to stay at our place, and there's no rule that I have to be the one to go meet them! I hadn't gone to see Chin in two weeks, and she had nothing to eat, so how could I not go see her? I'm tired, too, going to take care of Chin and everything. And she's studying for her exam—do you even know how important this test is to her?"

"How long are you going to go on bringing food to a grown child, who doesn't even stop by when her grandmother is missing?"

"What would she do if she came? I told her not to come. We searched everywhere. What can we do when even the police can't find her? Do we go from door to door and ring the bells and ask, Is our mother here? What can Chin do when even the adults can't do anything? A student has to go to school. Do we all just stop doing what we do because Mother isn't here?"

"She's missing, not 'isn't here.'"

"So what do you want me to do? You yourself go to work!"

"What?" He picks up a golf club from a corner and is about to hurl it across the room.

"Hyong-chol!" Father is standing at the open door. Hyong-chol puts down the golf club. Father had come to Seoul for his birthday to make it more convenient for his children. If they'd celebrated his birthday, as planned, Mom would have said, "This is celebrating my birthday, too," sitting at the table in the traditional full-course Korean restaurant where his wife, weeks before, had made a reservation. But with Mom missing, Father's birthday went by without any celebration, and Aunt took charge of the summer ancestral rites.

He follows Father out.

"It's all my fault," Father says, turning around at his grand-daughter's bedroom door.

Hyong-chol is silent.

"Don't fight. I know what you're feeling. But fighting doesn't help anything. Your mom met me and had a hard life. But she is a kind person. So I'm sure she's at least alive. And if she's alive, we'll hear something."

Hyong-chol stays silent.

"I want to go home now." Father stares at him for a while, then enters the room. Looking at the closed door, Hyong-chol bites his lip, and heat flares in his chest. He rubs his chest with his hands. He's about to rub his face with his hands, as is his habit, but stops. He can feel Mom's gentle touch. Mom hated it when he rubbed his hands or slouched. If he did that in front of her, she immediately straightened his hands and shoulders. If he was about to duck his head, Mom slapped him on the back, telling him, "A man has to be dignified." He never became a prosecutor. Mom always called it his dream, but he hadn't understood that it had been Mom's dream, too. He only thought of it as a youthful wish that couldn't be achieved; it never occurred to him that he had deflated Mom's aspirations as well. He realizes that Mom has lived her entire life believing that she was the one who held him back from his dream. *I'm sorry, Mom, I didn't keep my promise.* His heart brims with the desire to do nothing but look after Mom when she's found. But he has already lost that chance.

He crumples to his knees on the living-room floor.

3

I'm Home

A YOUNG WOMAN is peeking in, standing in front of the firmly closed blue gate.

"Who are you?" When you clear your throat from behind her, the young woman turns around. She has a smooth forehead and hair tied neatly back, and her eyes shine in delight.

"Hello!" she says.

You just stare at her, and she smiles. "This is Auntie Park So-nyo's house, right?"

The nameplate of the long-empty house has only your name engraved on it. "Auntie Park So-nyo"—it's been a long time since you heard someone call your wife Auntie, not Grandma.

"What is it?"

"Isn't she home?"

You are quiet.

"Is she really missing?"

You gaze at the young woman. "Who are you?"

"Oh, I'm Hong Tae-hee, from Hope House in Namsan-dong."

Hong Tae-hee? Hope House?

"It's an orphanage. I was worried because she hadn't stopped by in so long, and I came across this." The woman shows you the newspaper ad your son created. "I've come by a couple of times, wondering what happened, but the gate was always locked. I thought I would have to go away empty-handed today, too. . . . I just wanted to hear what happened. I was supposed to read her a book. . . ."

You pick up the rock in front of the gate, take the key out from its hiding place, and unlock the gate. Pushing open the gate of the long-vacant house, you look in, hopeful. But it's silent inside.

You let Hong Tae-hee in. Supposed to read her a book? To your wife? You have never heard your wife mention Hope House or Hong Tae-hee. Hong Tae-hee calls out for your wife as soon as she sets foot inside the gate, as if she can't believe that your wife is really missing. When there's no response, Tae-hee's expression grows cautious. "Did she leave home?"

"No, she's missing."

"What?"

"She went missing in Seoul."

"Really?" Tae-hee's eyes grow wide. She tells you that, for more than ten years, your wife came to Hope House and bathed the children and did the laundry and tended the garden in the yard.

Your wife?

Tae-hee says that your wife is highly respected and that she donates 450,000 won a month to Hope House. She explains that your wife has always donated this amount.

Four hundred fifty thousand a month?

Every month, your children in Seoul would pool together six hundred thousand won and send it to your wife. They seemed to think that two people could survive on that amount in the countryside. It wasn't a small sum. At first, your wife shared this money with you, but at some point she said she would take the entire amount. You wondered where this came from all of a sudden, but your wife asked you not to question how she was using the money. She said she had the right to use the money, since she was the one who had raised all the children. It seemed that she had thought about it for a long time. Otherwise, she wouldn't have said, "I feel that I have the right to use the money." That wasn't the kind of thing your wife would say. It sounded like something from a television drama. Your wife would have practiced that sentence by herself for a few days, into the air.

One Parents' Day in May, years ago, none of the children called. Your wife went to the stationery store in town and bought two carnation buds, each tied to a ribbon that said "Thank you for giving me life and raising me." She found you standing by the new road and urged you to come home. "What if someone sees us?" You followed her home. She persuaded you to come inside and lock the door, then pinned a carnation to the front of your jacket. "What would people say if we went around without a flower pinned to our clothes, when everyone knows how many children we have? That's why I bought these." Your wife fastened a flower on her clothes, too. The flower kept drooping, so she repinned it twice. You took off the flower as soon as you left the house again, but your wife went around the whole day with the flower on her chest.

The next day, she took to her bed, ill. She tossed and turned for a few nights, then sat up abruptly and asked you to transfer three majigi of land to her name. You asked her why, and she said it was because her life was pointless. She felt useless now that all the children had gone their separate ways. When you explained that all of your land is her land, too, and that if only three majigi were transferred to Park So-nyo she would lose out, because this would make it clear that the rest was yours, she looked disappointed and said, "I guess that's true."

But she was firm when she announced that she wanted all of the children's money. You didn't feel like going against her when she was like that; you thought you would get into a big fight if you did. You agreed on one condition: she could take all the money, but she couldn't come to you for more. Your wife said that would be fine. It didn't seem she was buying clothes or doing anything in particular with the money, but when you took a peek at the account books, 450,000 won was taken out of the bank account on the same day every month, in one lump sum. If the money came late, she called Chi-hon, who was in charge of collecting it from her siblings and sending it, to remind her to send the money. This, too, was unlike your wife. You didn't ask her what she was doing with it, because you promised you wouldn't, but you thought she was taking the 450,000 won every month to put in a savings account, to create purpose in her life again. You once searched for a savings-account passbook, but you never found one. If Hong Tae-hee is right, your wife had been donating 450,000 won a month to Hope House in Namsan-dong. You feel bludgeoned by your wife.

Hong Tae-hee tells you that it's really the kids who are waiting for your wife, more than she is. She tells you about a boy named Kyun, says that your wife practically became the boy's mother, that he was especially saddened that your wife had suddenly stopped coming to the orphanage. She says he was abandoned at the orphanage before he was six months old without even a name, but that your wife had named him Kyun.

"Did you say Kyun?"

"Yes, Kyun."

She says that Kyun is going to start middle school next year; your wife has promised to buy him a book bag and a uniform when he does. Kyun. A chill comes over your heart. You listen quietly to Hong Tae-hee's story. You can't believe you didn't know that your wife has been going to the orphanage for more than a decade. You wonder whether your missing wife could be the same woman Hong Tae-hee is talking about. When did she go to Hope House? Why didn't she say anything to you? You gaze at your wife's picture in Hong Tae-hee's newspaper ad and go into your room. From a photo album buried deep in a drawer, you peel off a picture of your wife. Your daughter and wife are standing at the pier on a beach, clutching their clothes, which are blowing astray in the wind. You push the picture toward Tae-hee. "Is this the person you're talking about?"

"Oh, it's Auntie!" Tae-hee calls out happily, as if your wife is standing in front of her. Your wife, her brow furrowed against the sun, is looking at you.

"You said you were supposed to read to her? What do you mean?"

"She did all the difficult work at Hope House. She particularly enjoyed bathing the children. She was so efficient that, after she came to visit, the whole orphanage would be sparkling clean. When I asked her what I could do to thank her, she said there was nothing, but one day she brought in a book and asked me to read it to her for an hour each time. She said it was a book she liked but that she couldn't read anymore, because of her bad eyesight."

You are quiet.

"It's this book."

You stare at the book Hong Tae-hee takes out of her bag. Your daughter's book.

"The author is from this area. I heard she went to elementary and middle school here. I think that's why Auntie likes this author. The last book I read her was by this author, too."

You take your daughter's book, *To Complete Love*. So your wife had wanted to read her daughter's novel. Your wife had never told you as much. You had never even thought of reading your wife your daughter's books. Does anyone else in the family know that your wife can't read? You remember how your wife looked hurt, as if you had insulted her, the day you found out that she didn't know how to read. Your wife believed that you did everything you did because you looked down on her, because of her illiteracy—leaving home when you were younger, yelling at her at times, rudely replying to her questions, "Why do you want to know?" That wasn't why you did those things, but the more you denied it, the more she believed it to be true. You wonder if you did look down on her, unconsciously, as she insisted you did. You had no idea that a stranger was reading your daughter's novel to your wife. How hard your wife must have worked to hide from this young woman the fact that she didn't know how to read. Your wife, wanting so badly to read your daughter's novel, couldn't tell this young woman that the author was her daughter, but blamed her bad eyes and asked her to read it out loud. Your eyes sting. How was your wife able to restrain herself from bragging about her daughter to this young woman?

"Such a bad person."

"I'm sorry?" Hong Tae-hee stares at you, her eyes round, surprised.

If she wanted to read it that badly, she should have asked me to read it to her. You rub your dry, rough face with your hands. If your wife had asked you to read her the novel, would you have read it to her? Before she went missing, you spent your days without thinking about her. When you did think about her, it was to ask her to do something, or to blame her or ignore her. Habit can be a frightening thing. You spoke politely with others, but your words turned sullen toward your wife. Sometimes you even cursed at her. You acted as if it had been decreed that you couldn't speak politely to your wife. That's what you did.

"I'm home," you mumble to the empty house, after Hong Tae-hee leaves.

———

All you wanted in life was to leave this house—when you were young, after you were married, and even after you had children. The isolation you felt when it struck you that you would spend your entire life in this house, in this dull town stuck to the south of the country, in the place of your birth—when that happened, you left home without a word and wandered the country. And when ancestral rites came around, you returned home, as if following genetic orders. Then you left again, and only crawled back when you became ill. One day, after you recovered from some illness, you learned to ride a motorcycle. You left home again, with a woman who was not your wife on the back. There were times when you thought you would never return. You wanted to forge a different life and forget about this house and set out on your own. But you couldn't last more than three seasons away.

When the unfamiliar things away from home became commonplace, the things your wife grew and raised hovered before your eyes. Puppies, chickens, potatoes that kept coming out when they were dug up . . . and your children.

· · ·

Before you lost sight of your wife on the Seoul Station subway platform, she was merely your children's mother to you. She was like a steadfast tree, until you found yourself in a situation where you might not ever see her again—a tree that wouldn't go away unless it was chopped down or pulled out. After your children's mother went missing, you realized that it was your wife who was missing. Your wife, whom you'd forgotten about for fifty years, was present in your heart. Only after she disappeared did she come to you tangibly, as if you could reach out and touch her.

———

It's only now that you clearly see the condition your wife was in for the past two or three years. She had sunk into numbness, would find herself not remembering a thing. Sometimes she would be sitting by a very familiar road in town, unable to find her way home. She would look at a pot or a jar she'd used for fifty years, her eyes wondering, What is this for? She became careless with the housekeeping, with strands of hair all over the house, not swept away. There were times when she couldn't follow the plot of a television drama that she watched every day. She forgot the song she used to sing for decades, the one that started with "If you ask me what love is . . ." Sometimes your wife seemed not to remember who you were. Maybe even who she was.

But that wasn't how it was the whole time.

. . .

Your wife would remember some tiny detail, as if she'd recovered something from ever-evaporating water. One day she mentioned how you had once wrapped some money in newspaper and stuck the bundle on the doorjamb before you left home. She told you that, even though she hadn't said it then, she was grateful you'd left those bills for her. She said she didn't know how she would have survived if she hadn't discovered that newspaper-wrapped money. Another time, your wife reminded you that you needed to have a new family picture taken, because the most recent portrait didn't include your younger daughter's third baby, who was born in America.

Only now do you realize, painfully, that you turned a blind eye to your wife's confusion.

When your wife's headaches made her unconscious, you thought she was sleeping. You wished she wouldn't lie down with a cloth wrapped around her head and sleep wherever she wanted to. When she was flustered, unable to open the door, you actually told her to look where she was going. Having never thought that you had to take care of your wife, you couldn't understand that your wife's sense of time had become jumbled. When your wife prepared slop and poured it in the trough in the empty pigpen and sat next to it, calling the name of the pig you had raised when you were young, saying, "This time, have three piglets, not just one—that would be so nice," you thought she was joking. A long time ago, that pig had

had a litter of three piglets. Your wife had sold them to buy Hyong-chol a bicycle.

"Are you here? I'm home!" you call to the empty house, and pause to listen.

You expect your wife to shout a greeting—"You're home!"—but the house is quiet. Whenever you returned home and called, "I'm home!" your wife would, without fail, stick her face out from somewhere in the house.

Your wife wouldn't stop nagging you. "Why can't you stop drinking? You could live without me, but you can't live without alcohol. The children tell me they are worried about you, and you still can't kick the habit!" She would go on nagging even as she took care of him, handing him a glass of Japanese raisin tea. "If you come home drunk one more time, I'm going to leave you. Didn't the doctor tell you at the hospital, didn't he say that drinking was the worst thing for you? If you want to quit seeing this nice world, then keep drinking!"

This was how your wife despaired when you went out for lunch and had some drinks with friends, as if her whole world had turned upside down. You didn't know that one day you would miss your wife's nagging, which used to go in one ear and out the other.

But now you can't hear anything, even though you got off the train and went into a blood-sausage-soup house nearby and had a glass, just so you could hear that nagging when you got home.

You look at the doghouse next to the side-yard gate. Your

wife grew lonely when the old dog died, and you had gone into town and brought back another one. The dog would have made some kind of noise, but it's completely silent in your house. You don't see the chain; your sister must have taken the dog with her, having tired of coming by to feed it. You don't close the gate, but leave it wide open and walk into the yard to sit on the porch. When your wife went to Seoul by herself, you often sat on the porch like this. Your wife would call from Seoul to ask, "Have you eaten?" and you would ask, "When are you coming home?"

"Why? Do you miss me?"

You would say, "No, don't worry about me, just stay as long as you want this time." No matter what you said, after she heard you say, "When are you coming home?" your wife would return home, regardless of why she had gone to Seoul. When you chided your wife, "Why did you come back so soon? I told you to stay as long as you want!" she would reply, "Do you think I came for you? I came to feed the dog," and give you a look.

———

You returned home because of the things your wife grew and raised, even though coming home meant that you had to cast away the things you'd obtained in other places. When you walked in through this gate, your wife would be digging for sweet potatoes, or making yeast with a soiled towel wrapped around her head, watching over Hyong-chol at his desk. Your sister liked to say that your nomadic leanings stemmed from your youthful habit of not sleeping at home, to avoid being drafted into the military. Once, however, you actually went to the police station, because you were tired of hiding. Your uncle, a detective, and only five years older than you, sent you away. He said, "Even though our family is ruined, the eldest son of the eldest son has to survive." Despite the family's decline, you had to survive to maintain the family graveyard and oversee the ancestral rites. But that wasn't a good enough reason for your uncle to stick your forefinger in the straw cutter and slice off a knuckle: it wasn't you but your wife who looked after the family graveyard and took care of the ancestral rites each season. Was that why? Did you become a vagabond because you were forced to leave home and sleep outside, blanketed in dew? That might have been it. The habit of sleeping on the street could have been why you wandered away from home. When you slept at home, you were overcome by anxiety that someone would rush through the gate to grab you. Once, you even ran out of this house in the middle of the night, as if you were being chased.

One winter night, you came home and your children had suddenly grown up. Everyone was sleeping huddled together because it was so cold outside. Your wife took the rice bowl she had left in the warmest part of the room and put a small table draped with a cloth in front of you. There was a snowstorm that night. Your wife toasted seaweed on the brazier. The nutty smell of perilla oil woke your children one by one, and they crowded around you. You wrapped some rice with seaweed and put it in each child's mouth. You put some in your eldest son's and your second son's and your elder daughter's mouths. Even before you got to your younger daughter or the baby, Hyong-chol was already waiting for more. It took you longer to prepare the rice than it took your children to eat it. You grew frightened of your children's appetites. You wondered what to do with all of them. That was when you decided that you needed to forget about the outside world, that you couldn't leave this house again.

———

"I'm home!"

You open the bedroom door. The room is empty. A few towels are neatly folded in one corner of the room, where your wife left them before you headed to Seoul together. The water you took your pills with on the morning of your departure has evaporated from the glass you set on the floor. The clock on the wall shows that it is 3 p.m., and the shadows of bamboos lean into the room, which faces the back yard.

"I said I'm home," you say to yourself in the empty room, your shoulders slouched. What were you thinking? When you shook off your son, who vehemently disagreed with your coming home by yourself, and you took the morning train, a small corner of your heart nurtured the hope that when you walked in and called, "Are you here? I'm home!" your wife would greet you as in old times—"You're home!"—perhaps while she cleaned the room or trimmed vegetables in the shed or washed rice in the kitchen. You thought that might happen somehow. But the house is vacant. It feels deserted, having been left empty for so long.

. You get up and open all the doors in the house. "Are you in here?" you ask at each door. You open the doors to your bedroom and the guest room and the kitchen and the boiler room. It's the first time you've desperately searched for your wife. Did she look for you like this every time you left home? You blink your dry eyes and open the kitchen window, to look at the shed. "Are you in there?" But there's only the bare platform.

Sometimes you stood in this spot and watched your wife busily doing something in the shed, and she would look over at you even if you didn't call her. And she'd ask, "What? Do you need something?" If you said, "Where are my socks? I want to go into town," she would quickly peel off her rubber gloves and come inside to find your clothes for you.

You stare at the empty shed and murmur, "Hey . . . I'm hungry. I want to eat something."

When you said you wanted to eat something, your wife would stop what she was doing without hesitation and come to you and say, "I picked some fatsia in the hills; do you want some fatsia pancakes? Do you want to eat those?"—even if she had been slicing off the tops of peppers or folding sesame leaves or salting cabbage. Why didn't you know then that you had a peaceful and lucky life? How could you have taken what your wife did for you for granted, without ever once making her seaweed soup? One day your wife came back from town and said, "You know that butcher you like in the market? I was passing by today, and his wife kept calling me, so I went in, and she invited me to share some seaweed soup, so I asked, 'What's the occasion?' She said it was her birthday, and her

husband had made her the soup that morning." You just listened, and she said, "It wasn't particularly tasty. But for the
first time, I was envious of the butcher's wife."

Where are you . . . ? If your wife would just come back, you
would make not only seaweed soup but also pancakes for her.
Are you punishing me . . . ? Water pools in your eyes.

You left this house whenever you wanted to, and came
back at your whim, and you never once thought that your
wife would be the one to leave.

———

Only after your wife went missing did you recall the first
time you saw her. It was after the families had decided that the
two of you would marry, before you had met each other.
The war was over, thanks to the cease-fire agreement between
the UN commander and the communist commander at Pan-
munjom, but the world was more unsettled than it had been
during the war. During this time, hungry North Korean soldiers came out of hiding in the hills at night and ransacked villages. When night fell, people with daughters of marriageable
age were busy hiding them. A rumor that the soldiers from the
hills snatched young women spread throughout the villages.
Some would dig holes near the railroad tracks and hide their
daughters there. Others spent the night huddled in one house
together. Some quickly married off their daughters. Your
wife lived in Chinmoe from her birth until she married you.
You were twenty years old when your sister told you that you

would be marrying a young woman from Chinmoe within a month. She said it was a young lady whose horoscope matched yours perfectly. Chinmoe. It was a mountain village about ten ri away from your village. In those days, it was common for people to marry without ever having glimpsed each other's faces. The ceremony was to be held in October in the yard of the young lady's house, soon after rice stalks were gathered from the paddies. Once the ceremony date was set, people teased you if you smiled, saying that you must be happy to be getting married. You neither liked nor disliked the idea. Because your sister did all of the housework in your house, everyone said you had to hurry up and get married. It made sense, but it occurred to you that you couldn't live with a woman you'd never even laid eyes on.

You never wanted to live your entire life farming in this village. At a time when there were so few people available to work that even children were called to the fields, you wandered around town with friends. You made plans to run away and set up a brewery in a city with two friends. You were preoccupied not with marriage but with how to raise the money to open a brewery, so what was it that made you head over to Chinmoe?

Your bride's house was a cottage embraced by a thicket of bamboo trees in the back, with ripe red persimmons hanging low on a tree in one corner. Your bride, wearing a cotton chogori, was sitting on the porch of the cottage, embroidering a phoenix on an embroidery frame. Bright light bounced off the roof and the yard, but the young woman's expression was dark. She looked up at the clear autumn sky once in a while, craning her neck. She watched some geese flying in a row until they disappeared. The young woman got up and left the porch. Unseen, you followed her to the cotton fields. Your future mother-in-law was squatting in the fields, picking cotton. The young woman called from afar, "Mom!" Your future mother-in-law answered, "What?" without looking up, continuing to pick cotton. White cotton danced in the brisk air. You were about to turn back, but something made you inch closer to the women and hide, crouching amid the white tufts. The young woman called "Mom!" again. Your future mother-in-law replied, "What?" without looking.

"Do I have to get married?"

You held your breath.

"What?"

"Can't I just live with you?"

Cotton blossoms waved in the breeze.

"No."

"Why not?" The young woman had sorrow in her voice.

"Do you want to be dragged off by the mountain people?"

Your bride was silent for a moment, then crumpled in the cotton field, her legs stretched out, and burst into tears. At that moment, she wasn't the well-groomed, demure woman who had been embroidering on the porch of the cottage. She wept so achingly that you wanted to cry, too, just from watching her. That was when your future mother-in-law waded out of the cotton fields and went to the young woman.

"Look, you're feeling this way because you're still young. I would have kept you by me a few more years if it wasn't for the war. But what can we do when the world is so frightening? It's not a bad thing to get married. It's something you can't avoid. You were born deep in the mountains. I wasn't able to send you to school, so if you don't get married what can you do? When I matched your horoscope with the groom's, it said that you two will be very lucky. You won't lose a single child, and you will have many children, and they will grow up and succeed. What else could you want? Since you came into this world as a human, you have to live happily with your mate. You have to have your babies and breastfeed them and raise them. Stop crying, stop crying. I'll make you special blankets with willowed cotton."

The young woman kept sobbing loudly, and your future mother-in-law slapped her on the back. "Stop, stop crying . . ."

Your bride didn't stop, and your future mother-in-law burst into tears, too.

If by pure coincidence you hadn't seen the two women crying in each other's arms in the cotton field, you might have left home before October. When you thought of that young woman, however, embroidering on the porch of the cottage, calling out "Mom!" at the cotton field, when you thought she might be dragged away by a soldier into the mountains, never to be seen again, you couldn't pick up your feet to go away.

———

When you came back to the empty house after your wife went missing, you slept for three days. You couldn't fall asleep at Hyong-chol's; at night you lay there with your eyes closed. Your hearing grew so sensitive that your eyes would fly open if someone came out of the room across the way to go to the bathroom. At each mealtime, you sat at the table for the others' sake, even though you weren't hungry, but in your empty house you didn't eat anything and slept like the dead.

You thought you didn't love your wife very much, because you married her after seeing her only once, but every time you left home and some time passed, she reappeared in your thoughts. Your wife's hands could nurture any life. Your family didn't have much luck with animals. Before your wife became a member of the family, any dog you got would die before giving you a litter. It would eat rat poison and fall into the toilet. Once, without anyone's realizing that the dog had crawled into the floor heater, a fire was kindled in the furnace, and not until you smelled the stench did you lift open the lid and pull out the dead dog. Your sister said that your family should not have a dog, but your wife brought home a newborn pup from the neighbors, one of her hands covering its eyes. Your wife believed that dogs, being smart, would return to their mothers if their eyes were not covered when they were taken away. Your wife fed that puppy under the porch, and it grew and had five or six litters. Sometimes there were as many as eighteen squirming puppies under the porch. In the spring, your wife coaxed the chicken to sit on eggs and managed to raise thirty or forty chicks without killing them, except a few that were snatched by a kite.

When your wife sprinkled seeds in the vegetable garden, green leaves shot up in a riot, more quickly than she could pluck the tender shoots to eat. She planted and harvested potatoes then carrots then sweet potatoes. When she planted seedlings of eggplant, purple eggplants hung everywhere throughout the summer and into the fall. Anything she touched grew in profusion. Your wife didn't have time to take the sweat-soaked towel off her head. As soon as weeds poked up from the fields, your wife's hands pulled them out, and she chopped the food waste from the table into small pieces and poured them into the puppies' bowls. She caught frogs and boiled them and mashed them to feed the chickens, and collected chicken waste and buried it in the vegetable garden, over and over again. Everything your wife touched became fertile and bloomed, grew and bore fruit. Her talent was such that even your sister, who endlessly found fault with your wife, would call her and ask her for help sowing the fields and planting pepper seedlings.

———

On the third night after you return home, you wake up in the middle of the night and lie still, staring at the ceiling. What is that? You're staring at a box with a yin-yang symbol, perched on top of the wardrobe, and quickly get up. Memories of your wife waking one day in the early dawn, stirring, and calling you, flood in. You didn't answer, even though you were awake, because you couldn't be bothered.

"You must be sleeping." Your wife heaved a deep sigh. "Please don't live longer than me."

You remained quiet.

"I have your shroud all prepared. It's in that yin-yang box on top of the wardrobe. Mine is in there, too. If I go first, don't panic, take that down first. I splurged a little. I got them in the best hemp. They said they planted the hemp themselves and wove the fabric out of it. You will be amazed when you see it—it's beautiful," your wife murmured as if she were casting a spell, even though she didn't know if you were listening.

"When Tamyang Aunt passed away a while ago, her husband was bathed in tears. He said that before Tamyang Aunt died she made him promise he wouldn't get an expensive shroud for her. She told him that she had ironed her wedding hanbok and asked him to put that on her when he sent her off to the next world. She said she was sorry that she was going first, without even seeing their daughter get married, and that he shouldn't spend money on her. Tamyang Uncle was leaning on me when he told me that, and he cried so much that my clothes got completely wet. He said that all he did was to make her work hard. That it was wrong of her to die, now that they were a bit more comfortable, and that she'd made him promise he wouldn't buy her a nice outfit even at her death. I don't want to do that. I want to go wearing nice clothes. Do you want to see them?"

When you didn't move, your wife sighed deeply again.

"You should go before me. I think that's for the best. They say that although there's an order to when people come into this world, there isn't one when you leave, but we should go in the order we came. Since you're three years older than me, you should leave three years earlier. If you don't like that, you can go three days earlier. I can just live here, and if I really can't live by myself, I can go to Hyong-chol's and be useful—peel garlic and clean—but what would you do? You don't know how to do anything. Someone has waited on you all your life. I can just see it. Nobody likes a smelly, silent old man taking up space. We are now burdens to the children, who have no use for us. People say you can tell from the outside a house that has an old person living in it. They say it smells. A woman can somehow take care of herself and live, but a man becomes pathetic if he lives alone. Even if you want to live longer, at least don't live longer than me. I'll give you a good burial and follow you there—I can do that."

You climb on a chair to take down the box from the top of the wardrobe. Actually, there are two boxes. From its size, it looks like the box in front is yours and the one behind is your wife's. They are much larger than they looked when you were lying down. She said that she hadn't seen such beautiful fabric in her life, that she'd gone far to get it. You open the box, and there are hemp cloths, mourning clothes, wrapped in blindingly white cotton. You undo each knot. The hemp to cover the mattress, hemp to cover the blanket, hemp to wrap the feet, hemp to wrap the hands, all inside, in order. *You said you'd bury me first and then go. . . .* You blink and gaze at the pouches that would wrap around your and your wife's fingers and toes after your deaths.

———

Two girls run in through the side gate toward you, calling you, "Grandpa!" Tae-sop's children, who live near the creek. They soon wander away from you, looking around the house. They must be looking for your wife. Tae-sop, who is running a Chinese restaurant in Taejon, left his two children with his elderly mother, who was so old she could barely take care of herself, and never showed his face. Perhaps he isn't doing too well. Your wife always clucked her tongue when she saw the children, saying, "Even if Tae-sop is like that, what kind of person is Tae-sop's wife to do this?" Neighbors whispered that Tae-sop's wife and the restaurant's cook had run away together. Your wife was the person who made sure the children ate, not their own grandmother. Once, your wife saw that they hadn't eaten and brought them home to feed them breakfast; the next morning, the girls came over, sleep still in their eyes. Your wife placed two more spoons on the table and seated the girls; after that, they came by at each mealtime. Sometimes they would arrive before the food was ready and go lie on their stomachs and play, and when the table was set they would run over and sit down. They stuffed their mouths as if they would never see food again. You were flabbergasted, but your wife took their side, as if they were her secret granddaughters: "They must be so hungry to do that. It's not like before, when things were difficult for us. . . . It's nice to have them around, it's not as lonely."

After the girls started to come for meals, your wife would, even in the morning, cook an eggplant dish and steam mackerel. When your children visited from Seoul with fruit or cake, she saved the treats until the girls poked their heads through the gate, around four in the afternoon. Soon enough, the girls started expecting snacks on top of three meals, and your wife also started to assume that she would feed them. You don't know how she managed to feed the children when Pyong-sik, the owner of the store in town, had to bring her home because he found her sitting at the bus stop, not knowing which bus to take home. Or when she left to go to the garden to pick some adlay but was found sitting in the fields beyond the railroad by Ok-chol. What did the children eat during your absence? You didn't think of the girls while you were in Seoul.

"Where's Grandma, Grandpa?" the elder child asks you, figuring out that your wife isn't here only after she has looked by the well and in the shed and the back yard and even opened the doors to the bedrooms. It's the elder who asks the question, but the younger girl comes right up next to you, waiting for your answer. You want to ask the same thing. Really, where is she? Is she even in this world? You tell the children to wait, and you scoop some rice from the rice jar and wash it and put it in the electric rice-cooker. The girls run around, opening every bedroom door. As if your wife might walk out of one of the rooms. You pause, not knowing how much water to pour in, because you've never done this before; then you add about half a cup more and press the switch down.

That day, in the subway car leaving Seoul Station, how many minutes did it take you to grasp that your wife wasn't there, in the moving subway car? You assumed that she had gotten on behind you. As the car stopped at Namyong Station and left it, you felt a sudden terror. Before you could examine the source of that feeling, something, despair that you had committed a grievous mistake that you couldn't go back on, punched your soul. Your heart was beating so loudly that you could hear it. You were afraid to look behind you. The moment when you had to confirm that you'd left your wife in Seoul Station, that you'd boarded the train and traveled one stop away, the moment that you turned around, accidentally hitting the shoulder of the person next to you, you realized that your life had been irreparably damaged. It didn't take even a minute to realize that your life had veered off track because of your speedy gait, because of your habit of always walking in front of your wife during all those years of marriage, first when you were young, then old, for fifty years. If you had turned around to check whether she was there right as you got on the car, would things have turned out this way? For years your wife used to make comments—your wife, who always lagged behind when you went somewhere together, would follow you with sweat beaded on her forehead, grumbling from behind—"I wish you'd go a little slower, I wish you'd go at my pace. What's the rush?" If you finally stopped to wait for her, she would smile in embarrassment and say, "I walk too slowly, right?"

She would tell you, "I'm sorry, but what would people say if they saw us? If they saw us, who live together, but one person is all the way up there and the other person is all the way back here, they would say, Those people must hate each other so much that they can't even walk next to each other. It's not good to appear that way to other people. I won't try to hold your hand or anything, so let's just go slower. What are you going to do if you lose sight of me?"

She must have known what would happen. The thing your wife said to you most frequently, ever since you met her when you were twenty, was to walk more slowly. How could you have not gone slower, when your wife asked you to slow down your entire lives? You'd stopped and waited for her, but you'd never walked next to her, conversing with her, as she wanted—not even once.

Since your wife has gone missing, your heart feels as if it will explode every time you think about your fast gait.

You walked in front of your wife your entire life. Sometimes you would turn a corner without even looking back. When your wife called you from far behind, you would grumble at her, asking her why she was walking so slowly. And so fifty years passed. When you waited for her, she stopped next to you, her cheeks reddened, saying with a smile, "I still wish you'd go a little slower." You assumed that was how you would live out the rest of your days. But since that day in Seoul Station when you left on the subway train, that day when she was only a few steps behind you, your wife still hasn't come to you.

You raise your leg, the one that was operated on for arthritis, and prop it on the porch, watching the girls wolf down the undercooked rice with only kimchi as panchan. After the surgery, you no longer felt pain or had circulation problems, but your left leg became impossible to bend.

"Want me to put a hot pad on it?"

You can almost hear your wife say that. Her hands dotted with dark sunspots, her hands that would put a pot of water on the stove and dampen a towel with the hot water and place it on your knee even if you didn't answer. Every time you saw her unshapely hands pressing down on the towel on your knee, you hoped that she would live at least one day longer than you. You hoped that, after you died, your wife's hands would close your eyes one last time, wipe down your cooling body in front of your children, and put the shroud on you.

"Where are you?" you, whose wife is missing, who's left behind, shout, your leg stretched out on the porch of the empty house, the girls having run off after they finished eating. You shout, trying not to succumb to the sobs that have been climbing to the top of your throat since your wife went missing. You couldn't scream or cry in front of your sons or daughters or daughters-in-law, but now, because of the rage or whatever it is, tears are pouring down your face, unstoppable. Tears that didn't come when your neighbors buried your parents, who died two days apart when cholera made the rounds in the village. Not yet ten years old, you couldn't cry, even though you wanted to. After your parents' burial, you walked down from the mountain, shivering, cold, and scared. Tears that didn't course down your face during the war. Your family used to own a cow. During the day, when South Korean soldiers were stationed in the village, you plowed the fields with that cow. In those days, North Korean soldiers would come down from the mountains into the village under cover of night and drag away people and cows. When the sun set, you would walk into town with the cow, tie it up next to the police station, and go to sleep leaning on the cow's stomach. At dawn you would bring the cow back to the village and plow the fields. One night, you didn't go to the police station, because you thought the North Korean soldiers had left the area, but they swarmed into the village and tried to drag the animal away. You wouldn't let go of the cow, even though they kicked you, beat you up. You ran after the cow, pushing aside your sister, who tried to block you from going, and even when you were beaten with the barrel of a rifle, you didn't cry. You, who didn't shed a tear when you were thrown into a water-logged rice paddy with other villagers, having been accused of being a reactionary because your uncle was a detective; you, who didn't cry when a bamboo spear went through your neck—you are sobbing loudly. You realize how selfish you were to wish that your wife survived you. It was your selfishness that made you deny that your wife had a serious illness. In some corner of your heart, you must have known that your wife, who often appeared fast asleep when you came home at night, kept her eyes closed because her headache was so severe. You just didn't think about it too hard. At a certain point, you knew that your wife would go outside to feed the dog, but instead would head for the well, or that she would leave the house to go somewhere but would stop in her tracks at the gate, not remembering where she was going, then give up and come back inside. You just watched as your wife crawled into the room, barely managing to find a pillow and lie down, a frown etched on her face. You were always the one in pain, and your wife was the one who looked after you. Once in a while, when your wife said her stomach hurt, you were the kind of person who would reply, "My back hurts." When you were sick, your wife put a hand on your forehead and rubbed your stomach and went to the pharmacy for medicine and made you mung-bean porridge, but when she wasn't feeling well, you just told her to take some medicine.

You realize that you've never even handed your wife a glass of warm water when she couldn't keep food down for days, her stomach upset.

It all started when you were roaming the country, immersed in playing traditional drums. Two weeks later, you came home, and your wife had given birth to your daughter. Your sister, who'd delivered the baby, said it was an easy birth, but your wife had diarrhea. It was so severe that she didn't have any color in her face, and her cheekbones were protruding sharply even though she had just had a baby. Her condition didn't improve. It seemed to you that she wouldn't get better unless you did something. You gave your sister some money for some Chinese medicine.

Your sobs grow louder as you sit on the porch of the empty house.

Now you see that this was the only time you've ever paid for medicine for your wife. Your sister bought three packets of Chinese medicine and boiled it and gave it to your wife. Afterward, when your wife had stomach problems, she would say, "If I could have had two more packets of Chinese medicine back then, I would have been cured."

Your relatives liked your wife. All you said to them was hello when they arrived and goodbye when they left, but your many relatives came because of your wife. People said that your wife's food brimmed with love. Even if all she did was to go to the garden and bring in some greens for bean-paste soup and a Chinese cabbage for a simple salted-cabbage dish, people dug in heartily, praising the bean-paste soup and the salted cabbage. Your nephews and nieces would come to stay with you during school vacations and comment that they had gained so much weight that they couldn't button their school uniforms. Everyone said that the rice your wife made fattened people. When you and your neighbors planted rice in your paddies and your wife brought them a lunch of rice and scabbard fish stewed with new potatoes, people would stop to stuff the food in their mouths. Even passersby would pause to eat. Villagers vied to help in your fields. They said that when they ate your wife's lunch they got so full that they could do double the amount of work before getting hungry again. If a peddler selling melon or clothing happened to peek inside the gate during the family's lunch, your wife was the kind of person who would welcome him in and give him a meal. Your wife, who happily ate with strangers, got along with everyone, except with your sister.

When your wife was suffering from stomach problems, she would complain as if that offense had occurred the day before. "It would have been good if I'd taken two more packets of Chinese medicine back then. . . . Even you said that I needed two more portions because I'd just had a baby and had to get well, but your sister said, with that mean face, 'Why do you need more medicine? This is enough.' And she didn't get me any more. If I'd taken two more portions I wouldn't have to go through this." But you had no recollection of it. And even though she repeated the story, you never got medicine for your wife when she had diarrhea.

"I should have taken more medicine. Now nothing works." When your wife had diarrhea, she stopped eating. You didn't understand how someone could stop eating for days. You ignored it when you were younger; not until you were older did you ever ask if she should eat something. Then your wife would say, with a miserable expression, "Animals don't eat when they're sick. Cows, pigs . . . when they're sick they stop eating. Even chickens. The dog stops eating when it's sick. When it's sick, it doesn't look at food, even if I give it something good, and it digs a hole in front of its house and lies down in there. A few days later, it'll get up. And that's when it will eat. People are the same way. My stomach is not feeling well, and even if the food is great, it's like poison when it gets inside me."

When the diarrhea didn't stop, she would grate dried persimmons and eat a spoonful. She would refuse to go to the hospital. "How can dried persimmons be medicine? Go to the hospital, and see the doctor, and get medicine from the pharmacy," you urged her, but she didn't listen. Finally, if you insisted, she would snap, "Didn't I say I wasn't going to the hospital?" and wouldn't let you bring it up again.

One year, you left home in the summer and returned in the winter, and when you got back you found a lump in your wife's left breast. You remarked that it wasn't normal, but your wife wasn't moved. Only when her nipple caved in and was filled with discharge did you take her to the hospital in town, her work towel still wrapped around her head. They couldn't tell you what it was right away, but examined her and said it would take ten days to get the results back. Your wife sighed. What happened during those ten days? What were you doing that was so important that you didn't go back to hear the results? Why did you put off going back to find out what was wrong? Finally, when her nipple became abscessed, you took your wife and went back to the hospital. The doctor said your wife had breast cancer.

"Cancer?" Your wife said that it was impossible: she didn't have time to lie in bed sick, she had too much to do. The doctor explained that your wife didn't fit the profile for a high risk of breast cancer. She hadn't had children late in life, she breast-fed all five children, she didn't get her period when she was very young, since she got it the year she married you, and she didn't enjoy meat—in fact, she couldn't afford to. But cancer cells were growing in your wife's left breast. If you had gone back to hear the results right away, they might not have had to cut off her breast. Soon after the surgery, her chest still wrapped with bandages, your wife planted potatoes in the field. Burying the sprouted potatoes in the field—which now belonged to someone else, because you'd sold it to pay for the surgery—she declared, "I will never go to the hospital again!" Not only did she refuse to go to the hospital, but she also wouldn't let you come near her.

Around the time you were to go to Seoul for your birthday, your wife was suffering from stomach problems. You worried whether she could go to Seoul if she was so weak, but she asked you to go to town to buy bananas, having heard about some remedy or other. Before you went to Seoul, she ate a mixture of two dried persimmons and half a banana for three meals straight. Even though she'd never stayed in bed for more than a week after giving birth, she was laid up in bed for ten days with the occasional stomach problem. And your wife started to forget the dates of ancestral rites. When she made kimchi, she would stop and sit staring into space. If you asked her what was wrong, she would say, "I don't know if I added garlic or not. . . ." She would pick up a boiling pot of fermented-bean-paste stew with her bare hands and burn them. You just thought, She's no longer young. You just thought, Even I spend my days without giving a thought to traditional drums, which I used to love so much. At this age, our bodies can't be the same. You just thought, It's about time things get broken. You assumed that ailments would be a constant companion at this age, and you thought that your wife was at that stage, too.

———

"Are you home?"

Your eyes fly open at your sister's voice. For a second, you think you hear your wife's voice, even though you know full well that only your sister would come to your house this early in the morning.

"I'm coming in," she says, and opens your bedroom door. Your sister is holding a tray laden with a bowl of rice and side dishes, covered in a white cloth. She places the tray on the floor at one end of the room and looks at you. She lived here with you until forty years ago, when she built a house by the new road, and ever since, she would get up at dawn, smoke a cigarette, smooth her hair and secure it with a hairpin, and come to your house. Your sister would walk around your house in the dawn light, and then go home. Your wife always heard your sister's footsteps, quietly circling the house, from the front yard to the side yard to the back yard. Your sister's footsteps were the sound that woke your wife. Your wife would grunt and turn over and mutter, "She's back," and get up. Your sister just circled your house and went home— perhaps she was checking to make sure that your house had remained intact overnight. When she was young, she lost two older brothers at the same time, and parents within two days of each other; during the war, she almost lost you. After she married, her husband came to live in your village, instead of your sister's going to live in her in-laws' village. The wound of losing her young husband in a house fire soon after was rooted deeply in your sister, and had grown into a large tree, one that couldn't be chopped down.

"Didn't you even bother to sleep on your mat?" Your sister's eyes, which used to be unfaltering and fierce when she was a young, childless widow, now look tired. Her hair, brushed neatly and secured with a hairpin, is completely white. She's eight years older than you, but her posture is straighter. She sits next to you, pulls out a cigarette, and puts it between her lips.

"Didn't you quit smoking?" you ask.

Without answering, your sister uses a lighter printed with the name of a bar in town and puffs on her cigarette. "The dog is at my house. You can bring it back if you want."

"Leave it there for now. I think I need to go back to Seoul."

"What are you going to do there?"

You don't reply.

"Why did you come back by yourself? You should have found her and brought her back!"

"I thought she might be waiting here."

"If she was, I would call you right away, wouldn't I?"

You're silent.

"How can you be like this, you useless human being! How can a husband lose his wife! How could you come back here like this, when that poor woman is out there somewhere?"

You gaze at your white-haired sister. You've never heard her talk about your wife in this way. Your sister always clucked her tongue disapprovingly at your wife. She nagged your wife for not getting pregnant till two years after your wedding, but when your wife had Hyong-chol, your sister was dismissive, saying, "It's not like she's done something nobody's ever done before." She lived with your family during the years when your wife had to pound grain in the wooden mortar for every meal, and she never once took over the mortar. But, then again, she helped take care of your wife after she gave birth.

"I wanted to tell her some things before I died. But who am I going to tell, since she's not here?" your sister says.

"What were you going to say?"

"It's not just one or two things. . . ."

"Are you talking about how mean you were to her?"

"Did she tell you I was mean to her?"

You just look at your sister, not even laughing. *Are you saying you weren't?* Everyone knew that your sister acted more like your wife's mother-in-law than her sister-in-law. Everyone thought so. Your sister hated hearing that. She would say that was how it had to be, since there was no elder in the family. And that might have been the case.

Your sister slips out another cigarette from her cigarette case and slides it in her mouth. You light it for her. Your wife's disappearance must have pushed your sister to take up smoking again. It was hard for you to think of your sister without a cigarette in her mouth. The first thing she did when she woke up every morning was to feel around for a cigarette, and all day long she looked for cigarettes before she did anything, before she had to go somewhere, before she ate, before she went to bed. You thought she smoked too much, but you never told her to quit. Actually, you couldn't tell her. When you saw her right after her husband died in the fire, she was staring at the house that had burned down, smoking. She was sitting there, smoking one cigarette after another, neither crying nor laughing. She smoked instead of eating or sleeping. Three months after the fire, you could smell cigarettes on her before you went near her, the tobacco seeped into her fingers.

"I won't live long now," your sister has said since the day she turned fifty. "All these years, I thought my lot in life was especially . . . especially harsh and sad. What do I have? No child, nothing. When our brothers were dying, I thought I should have died instead of them; but after our parents died, I could see you and Kyun, even though I was in shock. It seemed we were alone in the world. And then, since my husband died in the fire before I had a chance to grow fond of him . . . you're not only my brother, you're also my child. My child and my love . . ."

That would have been true.

Otherwise, when you were bedridden, half paralyzed from a stroke in your middle age, she couldn't have wandered the fields to harvest dew for a year, through spring, summer, fall, having heard that you would be cured if you drank a bowlful of dawn dew every day. To get a bowl of dew before the sun rose, your sister woke up in the middle of the night and waited for the day to break. Around that time, your wife stopped complaining about your sister and started treating her with respect, as if she were indeed her mother-in-law. Your wife, with an awed look on her face, would say, "I don't think I could do that much for you!"

"I wanted to say to her that I was sorry about three things before I died," your sister continues.

"What did you want to say?"

"That I was sorry about Kyun . . . and about the time I screamed at her for chopping down the apricot tree . . . and about not getting her medicine when she had stomach problems . . ."

Kyun. You don't reply.

Your sister gets up and points at the tray covered with the white cloth. "There's some food for you; eat it when you're hungry. Do you want it now?"

"No, I'm not hungry yet. I've just woken up." You stand, too.

You follow your sister as she walks around your house. Without your wife's caring hands, the place is covered in dust. Your sister wipes the dust off the jar lids as she walks by the back yard.

"Do you think Kyun went to heaven?" she asks suddenly.

"Why are you talking about him?"

"Kyun must be looking for her, too. I see him in my dreams all of a sudden. I wonder how he would have turned out if he'd lived."

"What do you mean, how he would have turned out? He'd be old, like you and me. . . ."

When your seventeen-year-old wife married twenty-year-old you, your little brother Kyun was in the sixth grade. A smart child, he stood out among his peers: he was sharp and outgoing and handsome and got good grades. When people passed Kyun, they turned around to take another look, wondering which lucky family had him as a son. But he couldn't go on to middle school because of your financial straits, although he begged you and your sister to let him go. You can almost hear it now: *Please send me to school, brother; please send me to school, sister.* He cried up a storm every day, asking you two to send him to school. Even though a few years had passed since the war, it was pitiable—you were unbelievably poor. Sometimes you think of those days as if they were a dream. You survived miraculously after being stabbed in the neck with a bamboo spear, but you were mired in a desperate situation as the eldest son of the extended family, responsible for feeding everyone. That might have been why you wanted to leave this house, because it was so difficult. It was difficult to find food, let alone send your brother to school. When you and your sister didn't listen to him, Kyun begged your wife.

"Sister-in-law, please send me to school. Please let me go to middle school. I'll spend my whole life making it up to you."

Your wife said to you, "Since he wants it so badly, shouldn't we send him to school somehow?"

"I couldn't go to school, either! At least he was able to go to elementary school," you retorted.

You couldn't go to school because of your father. As a doctor of Chinese medicine, he wouldn't let you go anywhere there were a lot of people, whether school or anyplace else, after he lost his two older sons to an epidemic. Your father, sitting knee to knee with you, taught you Chinese characters himself.

"Let's send him to school," your wife said.

"How?"

"We can sell the garden."

When your sister heard that, she said, "You're going to be the ruin of this family!" and she sent your wife to her hometown. Ten days later, drunk, your feet headed toward your in-laws' at night. You stumbled along the mountain path, and when you got to your in-laws' cottage, you stopped near the glowing window of the back room, the one closest to the bamboos. You didn't go there thinking you would bring your wife back. It was the rice wine that had brought you there, the makgoli you had been given after you helped a neighbor plow his fields. Even though you weren't the one who had sent your wife back to her childhood home, you couldn't step into your in-laws' house as if nothing had happened, so you just stood there, leaning against the dirt wall. You could hear your mother-in-law and your wife talking, just as you had in the cotton fields a short time ago. Your mother-in-law raised her voice and said, "Don't go back to that damn house! Just pack up your things and leave that family."

Your wife, sniffling, insisted, "Even if I die, I'm going to go back into that house. Why should I leave that house when it's my house, too?" You stood against the wall until the dawn light rippled into the bamboo forest. You grabbed your wife as she came out to make breakfast. She had cried all night, and her large, dark, guileless eyes were now so swollen they had become slits. You took your wife's hand and pushed through the bamboo woods, back to your house. When you got past the bamboo forest, you let go of your wife's hand and walked ahead of her. Dew dropped onto your pants. Your wife, falling back, followed you, breathing hard, saying, "Just go a little slower!"

When you got home, Kyun ran over to your wife, calling, "Sister-in-law!

"Sister-in-law," he said, "I promise I won't go to school. So don't leave like that again!" Kyun's eyes welled up; he had abandoned his dream. From that point on, Kyun, unable to go to middle school, threw himself into helping your wife and doing housework. When they worked in the hillside fields and Kyun couldn't see your wife behind the tall millet stalks, he would call out, "Sister-in-law!" When your wife said, "Yes?" Kyun would smile and call out again, "Sister-in-law!" Kyun would call and your wife would answer, and Kyun would call her again and she would answer him again. The two would finish up the work in the hills like that, calling and answering. Kyun was a faithful companion for your wife whenever you wandered from home. When Kyun got stronger, he plowed the fields with the cow in the spring, and harvested rice in the paddies in the fall, before anyone else. In the late fall, he went to the cabbage garden in the early morning and harvested all the cabbage. Back in those days, people hulled rice over straw mats on the paddies. Each woman would set up a brusher, a contraption of metal teeth in a four-legged wooden frame, and pull the stalks through, forcing the rice kernels off. All the village women owned such brushers, and they would go to the fields of the family who was harvesting that day and set these up. And they would thresh the grain until sunset. One year, Kyun, who had grown almost ten centimeters over the previous year, went to work at the brewery in town. With his first paycheck he bought a brusher, and brought it home to give to your wife.

"What's this brusher for?" your wife asked.

Kyun smiled. "Your brusher is the oldest in the village—it doesn't look like it can even stand on its own."

Your wife had told you that her brusher was so old that it took more effort for her than the other women to skim the grains, and had said she wanted a new one. Her words had gone in one ear and out the other. You thought, Her brusher is fine, what's the point of buying a new one? Holding the new brusher that Kyun had bought, your wife grew angry at Kyun, or maybe it was at you. "Why did you buy something like this, when we couldn't even send you to school?"

Kyun said, "It's nothing," and his face turned red.

Kyun got along well with your wife, perhaps thinking of her as his mother. After he bought the brusher, he brought home various things for the house whenever he had the money. They were all things that your wife needed. Kyun was the one who bought her a nickel basin. He explained, a bit embarrassed, "This is what the other women use, and my sister-in-law is the only one who uses a heavy rubber bin. . . ." Your wife made various kinds of kimchi in the nickel basin and used it to carry lunch to the fields. After she used it, she would polish it and put it up on top of the cupboards. She used it until the nickel wore off and the basin turned white.

You get up abruptly and go into the kitchen. You open the back door of the kitchen and look up at the shelf made of poles in the all-purpose room. Squat tables, their legs folded, are stacked on top. At the end sits the decades-old nickel basin.

You weren't home when your wife gave birth to your second son. Kyun was there with her. You heard what happened later. It was winter, and cold, but there was no firewood. For your wife, who was lying in a cold room after having given birth, Kyun chopped down the old apricot tree in the yard. He pushed the logs into the furnace under your wife's room and lit them. Your sister burst into your wife's room and scolded her, asking how she could do such a thing, since people say that family members will start dropping dead if you chop down a family's tree. Kyun yelled, "I did it! Why are you accusing her?" Your sister grabbed Kyun by the throat. "Did she tell you to chop it down? You bastard! You awful boy!" But Kyun refused to back down. His large, dark eyes glittered in his pale face. "Then do you want her to freeze to death in a cold room?" he asked. "Freeze to death after having a baby?"

Soon after that, Kyun left home to earn money. He was gone for four years. When he returned, penniless, your wife welcomed him back warmly. But Kyun had changed quite a bit while he was away. Though he had become a strapping young man, his eyes were no longer animated, and he appeared gloomy. When your wife asked him what he had done, and where he had gone, he wouldn't answer. He didn't even smile at her. You just thought the outside world had been unkind to him.

It was the spot where the apricot tree had stood. Maybe twenty days had passed since Kyun returned home. Your wife ran up to the store in town, where you were playing a game of yut, her face ashen. She insisted that there was something wrong with Kyun, that you had to come home right away, but you were immersed in your game and told her to go ahead. Your wife stood there for a moment, stunned, then flipped over the straw mat on which the yut game was set out. "He's dying!" she screamed. "He's dying! You have to come!"

Your wife was acting so strangely that you started for your house, a knot in your stomach.

"Hurry! Hurry!" your wife shouted, leading the way. It was the first time she had gone ahead of you, running. Kyun was lying on the spot where the apricot tree had stood. He was writhing, frothing at the mouth, and his tongue was hanging out.

"What's wrong with him?" You looked at your wife, but she was already overcome with grief.

It was your wife, who had found Kyun in that condition, who was called to the police station several times. Before they determined the cause of death, a rumor that she'd poisoned her brother-in-law with pesticide spread to the neighboring village. Your sister screamed at your wife, her eyes reddened, "You killed my baby brother!"

Your wife was calm as she was being questioned by the detectives. "If you think I killed him, then just put me away."

Once, the detective had to bring your wife home; she'd refused to leave the station, asking to be locked up in jail. Your wife would rip out her hair and grab at her chest in grief. She would bang open the door and run to the well and gulp down cold water. Meanwhile, you ran around in the hills and in the fields, crazed, calling the dead boy's name: *Kyun! Kyun!* The burning in your chest spread and you couldn't stand the heat in your body. *Kyun!* There was a time when the dead didn't speak and the ones left behind went crazy like that.

Now you realize how cowardly you were. You lived your entire life heaping all of your pain onto your wife. Kyun was your brother, yet your wife was the one who needed to be consoled. But because you refused to speak about it, you'd driven her into a corner.

Even though she was out of her mind with grief, it was your wife who managed to hire someone to bury Kyun. Years passed, but you never asked for the details.

"Don't you want to know where he's buried?" she would sometimes ask.

You wouldn't say a word. You didn't want to know.

"Don't resent him because he went like that. . . . You're his brother. And he doesn't have parents. So you have to visit him. I wish we could rebury him in a good spot in the ancestral graveyard."

You would yell, "Why do I need to know where that bastard is buried?"

Once, when the two of you were walking along some road, your wife stopped. She asked, "Kyun's burial spot is nearby; don't you want to go?" You pretended that you didn't hear her. Why had you hurt her like that? Until two years ago, on the anniversary of Kyun's death your wife would make food and take it to his grave. Coming down from the hills, she would smell like soju, her eyes red.

Your wife changed after that happened to Kyun. A formerly happy person, she stopped smiling. When she did smile, the smile quickly disappeared. She used to fall asleep as soon as she lay down, tired from her work in the fields, but now she would spend nights unable to sleep. She was never again able to sleep soundly until your younger daughter became a pharmacist and prescribed her some sleeping pills. Your poor wife, who couldn't even sleep. Maybe your missing wife still has undissolved sleeping pills stacked in her brain. The old house has been rebuilt twice since Kyun's death. Each time you rebuilt it, you threw away old things that had been stacked in a corner somewhere. But your wife took care of the nickel basin herself, worried that someone would lay hands on it. Perhaps she feared that, if it was mixed in with all the other items, she might never be able to find it. The nickel basin was the first thing she brought into the tent you lived in while the house was being rebuilt. When the house was done, before she did anything else, she would bring in the nickel basin and place it on a shelf of the new house.

Until your wife went missing, it didn't cross your mind that your silence about Kyun must have pained her. You thought, What is the point of talking about the past? When your daughter mentioned, "The doctor asked if there was anything that gave Mom a deep shock. Is there something I don't know about?" you shook your head. When she said, "The doctor recommended that she see a psychiatrist," you cut her off, retorting, "Who needs a psychiatrist?" You always thought of Kyun as something you had to forget about as you aged, and now it did feel as if you'd forgotten about him. After she turned fifty, even your wife said, "I don't see Kyun in my dreams anymore. Maybe now he's able to go to heaven." And you thought your wife was fine, as you were. Only in recent years did your wife start talking about Kyun again; you'd assumed she'd forgotten all about him.

One night a few months ago, your wife shook you awake. "Do you think Kyun wouldn't have done it if we'd sent him to school?" Then she whispered, almost to herself, "When I got married, Kyun was the nicest to me. . . . I was his sister-in-law, but I couldn't even send him to middle school, even though he wanted it so badly. I don't think he's been able to go to heaven yet."

You grunted and turned over, but your wife kept talking. "Why were you like that? Why didn't you send him to school? Didn't you feel bad for him when he was crying like that, wanting to go to school? He said he would find a way to continue if we just enrolled him."

You didn't want to talk to anyone about Kyun. Kyun was a scar upon your soul, too. Although the apricot tree was gone, you remembered clearly where he had died. You knew that your wife stared at that place sometimes. You didn't want to pick at your wound. There were worse things in life.

You clear your throat a few times.

Only after your wife went missing did you think that you should have spent some time that night talking candidly about Kyun with your wife. Kyun remained in your wife's heart as it grew emptier. In the middle of the night your wife would suddenly run out to the bathroom and crouch next to the toilet. She would put her hands out as if she were pushing someone away and scream, "It wasn't me, it wasn't me!" If you asked whether she'd had a nightmare, she would blink and stare at you blankly, as if she had forgotten what she was doing. That happened more and more frequently.

Why didn't you think about the fact that your wife had to keep going to the police station about Kyun? That she was rumored to have killed him? Why is it only now that you realize Kyun might have something to do with your wife's headaches? You should have listened to your wife, at least once. You should have let her say what she wanted to. The years of silence, after you had blamed it on her and didn't even let her talk about it—that pressure might have pushed your wife toward her pain. More and more frequently, you found your wife standing somewhere, lost. She would say, "I can't remember what I was going to do." Even though the headaches were sometimes so bad she could barely walk, she refused to go to the hospital. She insisted that you not tell the children about her headaches. "What's the point of telling them? They're busy."

When they did find out about them, she covered them up, saying, "I had one yesterday, but now I'm fine!" Once, she was sitting up in the middle of the night, and when you made a noise her face turned stone cold and she asked, "Why did you stay with me all these years?" Still, she continued to make sauces and pick wild Japanese plums to make plum juice. On Sundays, she rode on the back of your motorcycle to go to church, and sometimes she suggested going out to eat, saying she wanted to eat food someone else had cooked, at a place that served a lot of panchan. The family discussed consolidating all of the many ancestral rites into one day, but she said that she would do so when the time came for Hyong-chol's wife to take over the rites. Since she'd done the rites her whole life, she would continue to do them individually while she was alive. Unlike before, however, your wife would forget something for the ancestral-rite table and have to go to town four or five times. You just assumed that this was something that could happen to anyone.

———

The phone rings at dawn. *At this hour?* Filled with hope, you quickly pick up the phone.

"Father?"

It's your elder daughter.

"Father?"

"Yes."

"What took you so long to answer? Why didn't you answer your cell?"

"What's going on?"

"I was shocked when I called Hyong-chol's house yesterday. . . . Why did you go home? You should have told me. You can't leave like that and not pick up the phone."

Your daughter must have just found out that you came home.

"I was sleeping."

"Sleeping? The whole time?"

"I guess so."

"What are you going to do there by yourself?"

"Just in case she comes here."

Your daughter is quiet. You swallow, your throat dry.

"Should I come down?"

Of all the children, Chi-hon is the most energetic in looking for your wife. It's probably partly because she's single. The Yokchon-dong pharmacist was the last person to call to say he'd seen someone like your wife. Your son placed more newspaper ads, but there have been no more leads. Even the police said they'd done everything they could, and could only wait for someone to call, but your daughter went from emergency room to emergency room each night, checking on every patient without family.

"No . . . Just call if you hear anything."

"If you'd rather not be alone, come right back up, Father. Or ask Aunt to come stay with you."

Your daughter's voice sounds strange. As if she has been drinking. It sounds as if she's slurring her words.

"Have you been drinking?"

"Just a couple of drinks." She's about to hang up.

Drinking until these morning hours? You call her name

urgently. She answers, her voice low. Your hand holding the phone grows damp. Your legs give way. "That day, your mom wasn't well enough to go to Seoul. We shouldn't have gone to Seoul. . . . The day before, she had a headache and rested her head in a basin filled with ice. She couldn't hear anyone calling her. At night, I found her with her head in the freezer. She was in a lot of pain. Even though she forgot to make breakfast, she said we had to go to Seoul—you were all waiting for us. But I should have said no. I think my judgment is getting worse because I'm old. One part of me thought, this time in Seoul, we would force her to go to the hospital. . . . And with someone like that, I should have held on to her. . . . I didn't treat her like a sick person, and as soon as we got to Seoul I just walked ahead. . . . My old habit just took over. That's how it happened." The words you couldn't say to your children spill out of your mouth.

"Father . . ."

You listen.

"I think everyone's forgotten about Mom. Nobody's calling. Do you know why Mom had such a headache that day? It's because I was a bitch. She said so." Your daughter's voice slurs.

"Your mom did?"

"Yes . . . I didn't think I could come to the birthday party, so I called from China and asked what she was doing, and she said she was pouring liquor into a bottle. For the youngest. You know he likes to drink. I don't know. It wasn't even worth it, but I got so angry. He really has to quit drinking. . . . Mom was bringing it because it's something her baby likes. So I said to Mom, Don't take that heavy thing; if he drinks it and makes a scene, it's going to be your fault, so please be smart about it. Mom said, weakly, You're right, and said she would go into town and get some rice cakes—she always brings rice cakes for your birthday. So I said, Don't, nobody eats those rice cakes anyway, and we just take them home and put them in the freezer. I told her not to act like a country bumpkin, she should just go to Seoul without bringing anything. She asked me if I really stuck all the rice cakes in the freezer, so I said, Yes, I even have some that are three years old. And she cried. I asked, Mom, are you crying? and she said, You're a bitch . . . I told her all that so things would be easier for her. When she called me a bitch, I think I went a little crazy. It was really hot in Beijing that day. I was so angry that I yelled, Fine, I hope you're happy that you have a bitch for a daughter! Okay, I'm a bitch! and hung up on her."

You're silent.

"Mom hates it when we yell . . . and we always yell at her. I was going to call and apologize, but I forgot, because I was doing a million things at once—eating and sightseeing and talking to people. If I had called and apologized, she wouldn't have had such a bad headache . . . and then she would have been able to follow you around."

Your daughter is crying.

"Chi-hon!"

She is quiet.

"Your mom was very proud of you."

"What?"

"If you were in the newspaper, she folded it and put it in

her bag and took it out and looked at it again and again—if she saw someone in town she took it out and bragged about you."

She's silent.

"If someone asked what her daughter did . . . she said you wrote words. Your mom asked a woman at the Hope House orphanage in Namsan-dong to read her your book. Your mom knew what you wrote. When that woman read to her, Mom's face brightened and she smiled. So, whatever happens, you have to keep writing well. There's always the right time to say something. . . . I lived my life without talking to your mom. Or I missed the chance, or I assumed she would know. Now I feel like I could say anything and everything but there's nobody to listen to me. Chi-hon?"

"Yes?"

"Please . . . please look after your mom."

You press the phone closer to your ear, listening to your daughter's forlorn cries. Her tears seem to trickle down the cord of your phone. Your face becomes marred with tears. Even if everyone in the world forgets, your daughter will remember. That your wife truly loved the world, and that you loved her.

4

Another Woman

THERE ARE SO MANY pine trees here.

How can there be a neighborhood like this in this city? It's hidden away so well. Did it snow a few days ago? There's snow on the trees. Let me see, there are three pine trees in front of your house. It's almost like that man planted them here for me to sit on. Oh, I can't believe I'm talking about him. I'm going to visit with you first and then go see him. I'll do that. I think I should do that.

The apartments and studios that your siblings live in all look the same to me. It's confusing which house is whose. How can everything be exactly the same? How do they all live in identical spaces like that? I think it would be nice if they lived in different-looking houses. Wouldn't it be nice to have a shed and an attic? Wouldn't it be nice to live in a house where the children have places to hide? You used to hide in the attic, away from your brothers, who wanted to send you on all sorts of errands. Now even in the countryside apartment buildings that look the same have sprouted up. Have you gone up on the roof of our house recently? You can see all the high-rise apartments in town from there. When you were growing up, our village didn't even have a bus route. It has to be worse in this busy city if it's like that even in the country. I just wish they didn't all look the same. They all look so identical that I can't figure out where to go. I can't find your brothers' homes or your sister's studio. That's my problem. In my eyes, all the entrances and doors look the same, but everyone manages to find their way home, even in the middle of the night. Even children.

But you're living here, where it's nice.

Where is this, by the way? Puam-dong in Chongno-gu, in Seoul . . . This here is Chongno-gu? Chongno-gu . . . Chongno-gu . . . Oh, Chongno-gu! The first house your eldest brother set up as a newlywed was in Chongno-gu. Tongsung-dong in Chongno-gu. He said, "Mother, this is Chongno-gu. It makes me happy every time I write my address. Chongno is the center of Seoul, and now I'm living here." He said, "A country hick has finally made it to Chongno." He called it Chongno-gu, but he lived in a tenement house crammed on a steep hill called something like Naksan. I was so out of breath when I went all the way up there. I thought, How can there be somewhere like this in this city? It feels more like the country than our hometown! But I'm saying the same thing here, where you live. How can there be a place like this in this city?

Last year, when you came back to Seoul after spending

three years abroad, you were disappointed that you couldn't even rent the apartment you used to live in with the money you had, but I guess you found this village here. This is just like a village in the country. There's a café and an art gallery, but there's a mill, too. I saw them making rice cakes. I watched for a long time, because it reminded me of the old days. Is it almost New Year's? There were a lot of people making those long, white rice cakes. Even in this city there's a village that makes those rice cakes near New Year's! At New Year's I would cart a big bucket of rice over to the mill to make rice cakes. I would blow on my frozen hands and wait for my turn.

It must be inconvenient, though, to live here with three children. And it must be a long commute for your husband to go to work in Sollung. Is there even a market nearby?

Once, you told me, "I feel like I buy a lot of stuff when I go to the market, but everything goes so quickly. I have to buy three Yoplaits if I want to give one to each kid. If I want to buy enough for three days, that's nine, Mom! It's scary. I buy this much, and then it's all gone." You held your arms out to show me how much. Of course, it's only normal, since you have three children.

Your eldest, his cheeks red from the cold, is about to lean his bicycle outside the gate when he is startled by something. He pushes through the gate, calling, "Mom!" Here you are, coming out the front door, wearing a gray cardigan and holding the baby.

"Mom! The bird!"

"The bird?"

"Yeah, in front of the gate!"

"What bird?"

The eldest is pointing at the gate without saying anything. You pull the hood of the baby's jacket over his head in case he gets cold and come out to the gate. A gray bird is on the ground in front of the gate. It has dark spots from its head to its wings. The wings look completely frozen, don't they? I can see you thinking about me as you look at the bird. By the way, honey, there are so many birds around your house. How can there be so many birds? These winter birds are circling your house, and they're not making a peep.

A few days ago, you watched a magpie shivering under your quince tree and, thinking that it was hungry, you went inside and crumbled some bread your kids were eating and sprinkled it under the tree. You were thinking about me then, too. Thinking about how I used to bring a bowl of old rice and scatter the kernels under the persimmon tree for the birds sitting on the naked winter branches. In the evening, more than twenty birds landed under the quince tree, where you had sprinkled the breadcrumbs. One bird had wings as big as your palm. From then on, you spread breadcrumbs under the quince tree every day for the hungry winter birds. But this bird is in front of the gate, not under the quince tree. I know what this bird is. It's a black-bellied plover. Strange—it's not a bird that flies around alone, so why is it here? It's a bird that has to be near the ocean. I saw this bird in Komso, where that man lived. I saw black-bellied plovers looking for something to eat on the mud flats at low tide.

.   .   .

You're standing still, in front of your gate, and the eldest shakes your arm. "Mom!"

You're silent.

"Is it dead?"

You don't answer. You just look at the bird, your face dark.

"Mom! Is the bird dead?" your daughter asks, running outside at the commotion, but you don't answer.

The phone is ringing.

"Mom, it's Auntie!"

It must be Chi-hon. You take the phone from your daughter.

Your face clouds over. "What are we supposed to do if you're leaving?"

Chi-hon must be taking a plane again. Tears well up. I think your lips are trembling, too. You suddenly yell into the phone, "You're all too much . . . too much!" Honey, you're not that kind of girl. Why are you yelling at your sister?

You even slam down the phone. That's what your sister does to you and to me. The phone rings again. You look at the phone for a long time, and when it doesn't stop, you pick it up.

"I'm sorry, sister." Your voice has calmed down now. You listen quietly to what your sister is saying on the phone. And then your face gets red. You yell again: "What? Santiago? For a month?" Your face flushes even more.

"Are you asking me if you can go? Why are you even asking, when you've already decided you're going? How can you do this?" Your hand holding the phone is shaking. "There was a dead bird in front of my gate today. I just have this bad feeling. I think something's happened to Mom! Why haven't we found her already? Why? And how can you go away? Why is everyone acting this way? Are you going to act like that, too? We don't know where Mom is in this freezing cold, and you're all doing whatever you feel like doing!"

Honey, calm down. You have to understand your sister. How can you say this to her when you know how she's been for the past several months?

"What? You want me to take care of it? Me? What do you think I can do with three kids? You're running away, right? Because it's dragging you down. You were always like that."

Honey, why are you doing this? You seemed to be doing fine. Now you've slammed down the phone, and you're sobbing. The baby is crying with you. The baby's nose gets red. Even his forehead. The girl is crying, too. The eldest comes out of his room and looks at the three of you crying. The phone rings again. You quickly pick up the phone.

"Sister . . ." Tears fall from your eyes. "Don't go! Don't go! Sister!"

In the end, she tries to soothe you. It's not working, so now she says she will come over. You put down the phone and sit there silently, looking down. The baby climbs onto your lap. You hug him. The girl touches your cheek. You pat her on the back. The eldest crouches over his math homework in front of you, to make you happy. You stroke his hair.

Chi-hon comes in, pushing through the open gate. "Oh, little Yun!" Chi-hon says, and takes the baby from you. The baby, who is shy around other people, struggles to get back to you from his aunt's embrace.

"Stay with me a little bit," Chi-hon says, as she tries to cuddle with the baby, but he bursts into tears. Chi-hon hands you the baby. Once in his mom's arms, the baby smiles at his aunt, tears still dangling from his eyelashes. Chi-hon shakes her head and strokes the baby's cheek. You sisters are sitting quietly together. Chi-hon, who came running over in this snow because she couldn't calm you over the phone, doesn't say anything now. She looks awful: her face is swollen, her eyes are puffy. She looks like she hasn't slept well in a while.

"Are you going to go?" you ask your sister after a long silence.

"I won't." Chi-hon lies on the sofa, facedown, as if she has just put down a heavy load. She's so tired that she can't control her body. Poor thing. She pretends she's strong, but she's all soft inside. What is she going to do, running herself into the ground like that?

"Sister! Are you sleeping?" You shake Chi-hon's shoulder but then pat her. You gaze at your sleeping sister. Even when you fought as children, you two would settle down soon enough. When I came in to scold you, you would be sleeping, holding hands. You go into your bedroom for a blanket and cover her with it. Chi-hon frowns. That child, so careless. How could she drive all this way when she's so tired?

"I'm sorry, sister . . . ," you murmur, and Chi-hon opens her eyes and looks at you.

Chi-hon says, as if she's talking to herself, "I met his

mother yesterday. The woman who would become my mother-in-law if we got married. She's living with her daughter. Her daughter runs a small restaurant called Swiss. She's single. Their mother's very small and gentle. She follows her daughter around everywhere, calling her Sister. The daughter feeds her mother and gets her to bed and washes her and says, 'What a good girl you are,' and so the mother started calling her Sister. His sister said to me, 'If it's because of our mom that you haven't gotten married yet, don't worry about it.' She told me that she was going to continue living with their mom, acting like her older sister. She's going on vacation in January, but she arranged for their mom to stay at a nursing home. So that's the only time I have to come and look in, when she's not here. His sister said that, for the past twenty years, she's taken a monthlong vacation in January, using the profits from the restaurant. She looked content, even though her own mom was calling her Sister. She just smiled and said, 'My mom raised me until now, and all that's happened is a role reversal—it's only fair.'"

She stops and looks at you. "Tell me something about Mom."

"About Mom?"

"Yes, something about Mom that only you know about."

"Name: Park So-nyo. Date of birth: July 24, 1938. Appearance: Short, salt-and-pepper permed hair, prominent cheekbones, last seen wearing a sky-blue shirt, a white jacket, and a beige pleated skirt. Last seen . . ."

Chi-hon's eyes get smaller and finally close, pushed toward sleep.

"I just don't get Mom. Only that she's missing," you say.

I have to go now, but I can't seem to make myself leave. The whole day has gone by while I was sitting here.

Oh no.

I knew this was going to happen. This is something that would happen in a comedy. My goodness, it's so chaotic. How can you laugh in this situation? Your eldest is saying something to you, putting his hat on over there. What is he saying? What? Oh, he wants to go to the ski slopes. You tell him he can't. You're telling him that, since your move back here, he hasn't been able to keep up in school, and that he has to study with Dad during this break to make sure he can catch up when school starts again. If he doesn't do that, it's going to be hard to do well in school. While you're talking to him, the baby, who's just learning to walk, is about to eat some rice that's fallen under the table. You must have eyes on your hands. You're talking to your eldest and looking at him, but your hands are taking away the dust-covered rice from the baby. The baby is about to burst into tears, but then clings to your legs. You fluidly grab the baby's hand as he is about to fall over, as you explain to your eldest why he has to study. Your eldest, looking around him, maybe not listening to you, yells, "I want to go back! I don't like it here!" The girl runs out of her room, calling, "Mom!" She's whining that her hair is tangled. She's asking you to braid her hair, quickly, because she has to go to cram school. Your hands are now fixing your daughter's hair. All the while you're talking to your eldest.

My, all three children are hanging from you now.

My dear daughter, you're listening to all three children at once. Your body is trained to the needs of the children. You seat your daughter at the table and brush her hair, and when the eldest says he still wants to go skiing, you tell him as a compromise that you will talk to his dad about it, and when the baby falls down, you quickly put the brush down to help him up and rub his nose, then you pick it back up and finish your daughter's hair.

Then you turn to look out the window. You see me sitting on the quince tree. Your eyes meet mine. You mumble, "I've never seen that bird before."

Your children look at me, too.

"Maybe it's related to the bird that was dead in front of the gate yesterday, Mom!" The girl grabs your hand.

"No . . . that bird didn't look like this."

"Yes, it did!"

Yesterday, you buried the dead bird under this quince tree. The eldest dug a hole, and the middle child made a wooden cross. The baby made a lot of noise. You picked up the bird and folded its wings as you slipped it into the hole that had been dug by the eldest, and your daughter said, "Amen!" Afterward, the girl called her dad at work and told him all about the burial. "I made him a wooden cross, too, Dad!"

The wind has knocked down the wooden cross.

Listening to your children's chatter, you come over to the window to take a better look at me. Your children follow you to the window and stare at me. Oh, stop looking at me, babies. I'm sorry. When you children were born, I cared more about your mom than about you three. The girl stares at me, her hair braided neatly. When you, my granddaughter, were born, your mom couldn't breastfeed you. When your older brother was born, she was discharged from the hospital in less than a week, but there were complications when she had you, and she stayed in the hospital for more than a month. I looked after your mom back then. When your other grandmother came to visit at the hospital, you cried and your grandmother told your mom to breastfeed you, to stop your crying. Watching your mom put you to her breast even though she didn't have any milk, I glared at you, just a newborn. I even sent your other grandmother away and grabbed you from your mom's arms and smacked your bottom. People say that when a baby is crying the paternal grandmother will say, "The baby is crying, you should feed her," and the maternal grandmother will say, "Why is that baby crying so much, making her mom so tired?" I was exactly like that. You couldn't have remembered it, but you liked your other grandmother more than me. When you saw me you said, "Hello, Grandmother!" But when you saw your other grandmother, you called out "Grandma!" and ran into her arms. I felt guilty every time, thinking you must know that I smacked your bottom soon after you were born.

You've grown so pretty.

Look at your thick head of black hair. Each of your braids is a fistful of hair. It's the same as when your mom was little. I was never able to braid your mom's hair. Your mom wanted long hair, but I always cut it in a bob. I didn't have time to seat her on my lap and brush her hair. Your mom must be playing out her childhood wishes for long braided hair through you. She's looking at me, but her hand is playing with your hair. Your mom's eyes are clouding over. Oh dear, she's thinking about me again.

Listen, dear. Can you hear me in all this noise? I came to apologize to you.

Please forgive me for the face I made when you came back to Seoul with the third baby in your arms. The day you looked at me with shock on your face, blurting out "Mom!" has been weighing on my heart. Why was it? Was it because you didn't plan to have a third baby? Or was it because you were embarrassed to tell me that you had a third baby, when your older sister wasn't even married yet? For whatever reason, you hid the fact that you'd had a third baby in that faraway land, instead suffering through morning sickness all by yourself, and only when you were about to give birth did you tell us that you were having a baby. I didn't do anything to help when you had the baby, but when you came back, I said to you, "What were you thinking? What were you thinking, three babies?"

I'm sorry, dear. I apologize to the baby and to you. It's your life, and you're my daughter, my daughter with the amazing ability to concentrate when you solve problems. Of course you would find a solution for your situation. I forgot who you were for a second and said that to you. I'm also sorry for all the faces I made without even knowing it, every time I saw you after you came back from America. You were so busy. I visited you once in a while, and you were always busy chasing after the children. You were picking up clothes, feeding them, pulling up a fallen child, taking the book bag of the child who came home from school, hugging the child who ran into your arms calling "Mom!" You were busy making things for the children to eat the day before you went into surgery to have a cyst removed from your womb. You wouldn't know how sad it made me, when I was at your house to look after the children and opened the door of the fridge. Four days' worth of the children's food was stacked neatly in the fridge. You explained to me, "Mom, give them the stuff on the top shelf tomorrow, then give them what's under that the next day . . . ," while your eyes were sunk deeply in your face. You are that kind of person. The kind of person who has to do everything with your own hands. That's why I said, "What were you thinking?" when you had the third baby. The night before your surgery, I picked up the clothes you'd taken off and left outside the bathroom while you took a shower. There were drops of plum juice on your shirt, which had frayed sleeves, and the seam of your baggy pants was ripped, and your old bra straps had millions of fuzzy bits on them, and I couldn't tell what pattern your rolled-up underwear used to have. Flowers or water drops or bears? It was speckled with color. You were always a neat and clean child, unlike your sister. You were the child who would wash your white sneakers if there was even a pea-sized smudge on them. I wondered why you'd studied so much, if you were going to live like this. My love, my daughter. When I thought about it, I did remember that you liked young children when you were little. You were the kind of child who would unhesitatingly give something you wanted to eat to a neighbor's child if it looked like he wanted it. Even when you were little, when you saw a child who was crying, you would go up to him and wipe his tears and give him a hug. I'd completely forgotten that you were like that. I was upset to see you wearing old clothes, with your hair tied back away from your face, busy and focused on raising kids, not even thinking about going back to work. I'm talking about the time I said to you, "How can you live like this?" while you were wiping the floor of the bedroom with a rag. Please forgive me for saying that. Although, back then, you didn't seem to understand what I was talking about. Finally, I just stopped visiting your house. I didn't want to see you living like that, when you had a good education and talent that others envied. My sweet daughter! You deal with what comes at you head on, without running away, and go forward with your life, but sometimes I was angry about the choice you'd made.

Honey.

Please remember that you were always a source of happiness for me. You're my fourth child. I never told you this, but, strictly speaking, you're my fifth child. Before you, there was a child who went to the other world as he was being born. Your aunt delivered the baby, and told me it was a boy, but the baby didn't cry. He didn't open his eyes, either. It was a stillbirth. Your aunt said she would hire someone to bury the dead baby, but I told her not to. Your father wasn't at home then. I lay in my room for four days with the dead baby. It was winter. At night, the falling snow was reflected on the mulberry paper of the window. On the fifth day, I got up and put the dead baby in a clay jar and carried it to the hills and buried him. The person who dug the frozen earth wasn't your father, but that man. If that baby hadn't been buried, you would have three older brothers. And then I gave birth to you by myself. Was there a reason for that? No. No. There was no reason. When I said I would have you by myself, your aunt was hurt. I'm only saying this now, but I was more scared of a dead baby coming out than going through childbirth alone. I didn't want to show that to anyone. If another dead baby came out, I wanted to bury it myself and not come down from the mountain. When I started having labor pains, I didn't tell your aunt, but brought hot water into my room and seated your sister, who was very young, by my head. I didn't even scream, because I didn't want to let anyone know in case a dead baby came out. But then out of me came you, warm and squirmy. When I slapped your bottom before wiping you clean, you burst into tears. Looking at you, your sister laughed. She said, "Baby," and patted your soft cheek with her palm. Drunk with your presence, I didn't even feel the pain. Later, I realized that my tongue was covered in blood. That's how you were born. You were the child that came into this world, the child that reassured me when I was stuck in sorrow and fear that another dead baby would be born.

Honey.

At least for you, I was able to do everything other moms did. I was able to breastfeed you for over eight months, because I had a lot of milk. I was able to send you to a place called kindergarten, which was a first for our family, and for your first shoes I was able to buy sneakers instead of rubber shoes. And, yes, I made your name tag when you went to school. Your name was the first letters I ever wrote. I practiced so much for that. I pinned on your chest a handkerchief and your name tag that I wrote myself, and took you myself to the school. You wonder why that's a big deal? It was a big deal for me. When Hyong-chol went to elementary school, I didn't go with him: in case I might have to write something, I made this or that excuse and sent him with your aunt. I can still hear your brother grumbling that everyone else's mom came but he had to go with his aunt. When your second-eldest brother went to school, I sent him with Hyong-chol. I sent your sister with Hyong-chol, too. For you and only you, I went to town and bought a schoolbag and a frilly dress. I was so happy that I was able to do that. Even though it was as small as a tray, I asked that man to build you a desk. Your sister didn't have a desk. She still talks about it sometimes, about how her shoulders got broader because she had to do her homework hunched over on the floor. It made me very proud to watch you sit there and study and read. When you were studying to get into college, I even packed you lunch. When you had study sessions at night, I waited for you at school and walked you home. And you made me very happy. You were the best student in our small town.

When you were accepted into a top university in Seoul, and into the pharmacy school at that, your high school hung a congratulatory placard in your honor. Whenever someone said to me, "Your daughter is so smart!" I'm sure my smile stretched up to my ears. You wouldn't know how proud I was to be your mother when I thought about you. I wasn't able to do anything for the others, and even though they are also my children, I never felt that way about them. I felt regretful and guilty, even though they were my children. You were the child who freed me from that feeling. Even when you went to college and ran around demonstrating, I didn't interfere, the way I did with your brothers. I didn't come to see you when you were on a hunger strike at that famous church they say is in Myongdong. When your face was covered in pimples, maybe because of the tear gas, I just left you alone. I thought, I don't know exactly what she's doing, but I'm sure she's doing it because she can do it. When you and your friends came down to the country and set up evening classes for the community, I cooked for you. Your aunt said you might become a red if I left you alone, but I let you talk and behave freely. I couldn't do that with your brothers. I tried to persuade them and I scolded them. When your second-eldest brother was beaten by riot policemen, I heated salt and placed it on his back to help him feel better, but I threatened to kill myself if he kept doing it. And all the while, I was scared that your brother would think I was stupid. I know there are things young people have to do when they're young, but I tried my hardest to stop the others from doing them. I didn't do that with you. Even though I didn't know what it was you were fighting to change, I didn't try to stop you. One year when you were in college—in June, remember—I even went with you to City Hall, following a funeral procession. That was when I was in Seoul because your niece was born.

I have a pretty good memory, don't I?

It's not a question of memory, though, because it was an

unforgettable day. For me, it was that kind of day. As you were leaving the house at dawn, you saw me and asked, "Mom, do you want to come?"

"Where?"

"Where your second son went to school."

"Why? It's not even your school."

"There's a funeral, Mom."

"Well . . . why would I go there?"

You stared at me and were about to close the door behind you, but you came back in. I was folding your newborn niece's diapers, and you yanked them out of my hands. "Come with me!"

"It's almost time for breakfast. I have to make seaweed soup for your sister-in-law."

"Will she die if she doesn't eat seaweed soup for one day?" you asked harshly, uncharacteristically, and forced me to change my clothes. "I just want to go with you, Mom. Come on!"

I liked those words. I still remember the tone of your voice as you, a college student, told me, who had never gone near a school, to come to school with you because "I just want to go with you, Mom."

That was the first time I saw so many people gathered like that. What was the name of that young man, who'd died after being hit by tear-gas pellets, who was only twenty years old? I asked you many times and you told me many times, but it's hard to remember. Who was that young man who caused so many people to gather? How could there be so many people? I followed you in the funeral procession to City Hall, and I looked for you and grabbed your hand again and again, afraid I might lose you. You told me, "Mom! If we lose sight of each other, don't walk around. Just stand still. Then we'll be able to find each other."

I don't know why I didn't remember that till now. I should have remembered it when I couldn't get on the subway car with your father in Seoul Station.

Honey, you gave me so many good memories like that. The songs you sang as you walked along holding my hand, the sound of all those people shouting the same chant—I couldn't understand it or follow it, but it was the first time I went to a plaza. I was proud of you for taking me there. You didn't seem like just my daughter. You looked very different from how you were at home—you were like a fierce falcon. I felt for the first time how resolute your lips were, and how firm your voice was. My love, my daughter. Every time I went to Seoul after that, you took me out, apart from the rest of the family, to the theater or to the royal tombs. You took me to a bookstore that sold music and put headphones over my ears. I learned through you that there was a place like Kwanghwamun in this Seoul, that there was something called City Hall Plaza, that there were movies and music in this world. I thought you would live a life different from the others. Since you were the only child who was free from poverty, all I wanted was for you to be free from everything. And with that freedom, you often showed me another world, so I wanted you to be even freer. I wanted you to be so free that you would live your life for other people.

.   .   .

I think I'll go now.

But, oh . . .

The baby looks sleepy. He's drooling and his eyes are half closed. Now that the two older children are at school, the house is quiet. But what is this? The house is a complete mess. My goodness, I've never seen such a messy house. I want to tidy it up for you . . . but now I can't. My daughter is drifting off as she gets the baby to sleep. Yes, you must be so tired. My baby is sleeping, curled around her baby. It's in the middle of winter, so why are you sweating so much? My love, my daughter. Please relax your face. You'll get wrinkles if you sleep with such a weary expression. Your youthful face is now gone. Your small, crescent-moon-like eyes have become smaller. Now, even when you smile, the cuteness of your youth is gone. Since I've lived to see you with wrinkles like this, I can't say my life has been short. Still, dear, I never could have guessed that you would be living like this, with three babies. You were so different from your emotional sister, who got angry quickly and cried and got sullen and turned blue in the face if things didn't work out her way. You created a schedule and you tried to follow it like you'd planned. When you said to me, "I didn't know, Mom, that I would have three kids, but when I became pregnant, I had to have the baby," you were so foreign to me. I thought your sister might be the one to have a lot of children. You never get angry. Of all my children, you are the only one who knows how to say things calmly, point by point, even to someone who is extremely angry. So that's why I thought you would weigh whether to have a child, and have only one. You never begged for anything, unlike your sister, who threw tantrums asking for a desk like the one your brothers had. I would ask you what you were doing as you bent over the floor, and you would say, "I'm doing my math homework." Your sister never even looked at a math book, but you were very good at it. You were the child with amazing concentration when it came to solving problems. When you came up with an answer, you would grin happily.

But you won't be able to find the answer to why this happened to me. That's why you must be in pain. Because of your three children, you can't go looking for me like you want to. You can only call your sister every evening and say, "Sister, was there any news about Mom today?" My love, my daughter. Because of your children, you couldn't look for me as much as you wanted to and couldn't weep as much as you pleased. I couldn't do for you as much as I wanted to recently, but I thought about you a lot when my mind was clear. About you, about how you have to raise three children, including the baby, who is just learning to walk, about your life. I felt regretful that the only thing I could do for you was to make kimchi and send some to you. My heart broke that time when you came to visit with the baby and said, with a smile, as you took your shoes off, "Oh, Mom, look, I've put on mismatched socks." How busy you must be if you, who have always been so neat, can't find the time to find a pair of matching socks. Sometimes when my mind was clear I thought of the things I had to do for you and your children. And it gave me the will to keep living . . . but then things turned out like this.

I want to take off these blue plastic sandals—the heels are

all worn down. And my dusty summer clothes. Now I want to get away from this unkempt way I look; I can't even recognize myself. My head feels like it's about to crack open. Now, dear. Raise your head a bit. I want to hold you. I'm going to go now. Lie down, put your head on my lap for a little while. Rest a bit. Don't be sad for me. I was happy so many days of my life because I had you.

———

Oh, you're here.

When I went to your house in Komso, the wooden gate facing the beach was broken and the bedroom door was locked; it must have been empty for a long time. Why did you lock the bedroom like that but leave the kitchen door wide open? The ocean wind had banged the wooden door open and shut so many times that it was half shattered.

But why are you in the hospital? And what is the doctor doing? He's not making you better, he keeps asking you silly questions. He keeps asking you your name. Why is he doing that? And why aren't you telling him your name? All you have to say is "Lee Eun-gyu," so why are you not answering, making him ask again and again? Really, why is the doctor doing that? Now he's holding a toy boat and asking, "Do you know what this is?" Is this a joke? It's a boat! What does he mean, "Do you know what this is?" But the strangest thing is you. Why aren't you answering? Oh, you really don't know? You mean you have forgotten what your name is? You don't know what that toy boat is? Really?

The doctor is asking again: "Your age?"

"One hundred!"

"No, please tell me how old you are."

"Two hundred!"

You're really being grumpy. Why do you say you are two hundred years old? You're five years younger than me, so that makes you . . . The doctor asks your name again.

"Shin Gu!"

"Please think carefully."

"Baek Il Sup!"

The actor Shin Gu? The television actor Baek Il Sup? Are you talking about the Shin Gu and Baek Il Sup that I like?

"Please don't do that, think and tell us what it is."

You're sniffling. What is going on? Why are you here, and why are you being asked these silly questions? Why are you crying, unable to answer these easy questions? I've never seen you cry before. I was always the one who cried. You saw me cry so many times, but this is the first time I'm seeing you cry.

"Now, please tell me your name again!"

You're quiet.

"One more time!"

"Park So-nyo!"

That's not your name, that's mine. I remember the day you asked me what my name was. You're paved in my heart like an old road. Like the pebbles in a pebble field, dirt in dirt, dust in dust, cobwebs in cobwebs. I was young then. I don't think I ever thought I was in my youth when I was living it, but if I think about when I first met you, I can see my youthful face. One late afternoon, I was walking home from the mill on the new avenue, kicking up dust, my nickel basin filled with flour resting on my head. My youthful footsteps were quick. I was on my way home to make dough out of the flour and cook dough-flake soup to feed the children. The mill was four or five ri away, across the bridge. My forehead was sweaty from the flour-filled nickel basin on my head. You passed by me on a bicycle, then stopped along the road and called, "Excuse me."

I kept walking, looking straight ahead. My breast was about to pop out of my chogori, which I was wearing with baggy pants.

"Put down that basin and give it to me. I'll carry it for you on my bicycle."

"How can I trust a stranger passing by and give this to you?" I said, but my youthful steps slowed. Actually, the basin was so heavy that my head felt like it would get crushed. I'd made a cushion out of a towel and put it under the basin, but I still felt as if my forehead and the bridge of my nose were going to collapse.

"I'm not carrying anything on my bike anyway. Where do you live?"

"In the village across the bridge . . ."

"There's a shop at the entrance to the village, right? I'll leave it there for you. So give it here and walk more freely. It looks so heavy, and here I am on a bicycle, carrying nothing on it. If you just put that basin down, you'll be able to walk faster and get home quicker."

I looked at you as you got off your bicycle, and I bit down on the end of the towel hanging by my face, the towel I'd placed on my head under the basin. Compared with Hyong-chol's father, you were plain-looking, both then and now. You were pale, like you had never worked a day in your life, and your long horselike face and drooping eyes weren't all that handsome. Your thick, straight eyebrows made you look honest. Your mouth made you seem respectable and trustworthy. Your eyes, gazing at me quietly, were familiar, as if I'd seen them somewhere before. When I didn't immediately give you the basin and instead studied your face, you turned to get back on your bicycle. "I don't have a hidden motive. I just wanted to help out because it looked so heavy. I can't force you to let me help you if you don't want me to." You placed a foot on the sturdy pedal of your bicycle. That was when I hurriedly thanked you and handed over the basin from my head. I watched as you undid the thick rubber ties on the back of the bicycle and secured the basin with them.

"So I'll leave it at the shop!"

You raced down the avenue—you, a man I'd just met, carrying my children's food. I took off the towel wrapped around my head and slapped the dust off my pants and watched you and your bicycle disappear. Dust rose and clouded you and your bicycle, so I rubbed my eyes and watched you get smaller. I felt relieved, the weight on my head gone. I walked along the avenue, swinging my arms lightly. A pleasant breeze passed through my clothes. When was the last time I'd walked alone, with nothing in my hands, on my head, or on my back? I looked up at the birds flying in the dusky sky, hummed a song

I used to sing with my mother when I was young, and headed to the shop. I looked for the basin from far away. I looked at the door of the shop as I approached it, but the basin that should have been by the door wasn't there. Suddenly my heart started beating fast. I walked faster. I was afraid to ask the woman at the shop, "Did anyone leave a basin for me?" If you had, I would have seen it already, but I couldn't find it. My towel in my hand, I ran toward the shopkeeper, who stared at me, wondering what was going on. I realized it only then: you had stolen my children's dinner from me. Tears filled my eyes. Why did I give my basin to a man I'd never seen before, trusting you? What was I thinking? Why did I do that? I can still feel that dread, when my momentary nervousness at seeing your bicycle disappear became reality. I couldn't go home empty-handed like that. I had to find that basin with flour, no matter what. I remembered the scraping noise I'd heard that morning when I scooped up grain in the shed for breakfast. I couldn't give up when I knew there was enough flour in that basin for ten days' worth of meals. I just kept walking, looking for you and your bicycle, though you must have sped past the shop. I went on and on, asking whoever I met whether they'd seen someone who looked like you. Your identity was revealed quickly. That was how careless you were. You didn't even live far away. When I found out that you lived in the village that had a tile-roofed house, about five ri past our village, before the road reached town, I started running. I would be able to bring back all of the flour in the basin if I reached you before you used it.

When I discovered your bicycle in front of a run-down

house at the foot of a hill between paddies, down the road from the entrance to your village, I ran into your house, screaming, "Ahhhh!" And then I saw it all. Your elderly mother sitting on the old porch, with her sunken eyes. Your three-year-old sucking on his finger. And your wife in the middle of a difficult birth. I'd come to retrieve the basin you'd stolen from me. Instead, I grabbed a pot off the wall in the dark and narrow kitchen. I heated water in it. I pushed you aside, since you didn't know what to do and were just hovering next to your wife, and I grabbed her hand. I'd never met her before, but I shouted at her, "Push! Push harder!" I don't know how much time passed until we heard the baby's cry. Your house didn't have a single strand of seaweed to make seaweed soup for your wife. Your elderly mother was blind and seemed already to be on her way over to the other world. I delivered the baby and scooped some flour from my basin and made dough for dough-flake soup and ladled it into a few bowls and put some broth into the room where the baby's mother was. How many decades ago was it when I put the basin back on my head and came home? Is that man next to you the baby who was born that day? He's sponging your hand. He gets you to turn over and sponges your back. It's been a long time. Your taut neck is now wrinkly. Your thick eyebrows are no longer, and I don't recognize your mouth. Instead of the doctor, it is now your son who says, "Father! What's your name? Do you know what your name is?"

"Park So-nyo."

No, that's my name.

"Who's Park So-nyo, Father?"

I'm curious about that, too. What am I to you? Who am I to you?

Seven or eight days after I met you, your situation weighing on my mind, I took a strand of seaweed and stopped by your house, but only the newborn was there, not your wife. You told me that your wife had suffered from three days of high fever after the birth, and finally left this world; she was so malnourished that she couldn't make it through childbirth. Your blind mother was sitting on the old porch, and it wasn't clear whether she knew what was going on. And the three-year-old. I suppose that man by your sickbed could be the three-year-old, not the baby.

I don't know who I was to you, but you were my lifelong friend. Who would have known that we would be friends all these years? The first time we met, you made me feel so despondent by stealing the basin with the flour I needed to feed my children. Our children wouldn't understand us. It would be easier for them to understand that hundreds of thousands of people died in the war than to understand you and me.

Even though I knew that your wife was gone, I couldn't just leave, so I soaked in water the seaweed I'd brought. I made dough from the remaining flour I'd given you the other day and made dough-flake soup with seaweed; I put a bowl for each person on the table and was about to leave, but stopped to put the newborn to my breast. It was a time when I didn't have enough milk for my own daughter. You were going around the village with the baby and feeding him donated breast milk. Life is sometimes amazingly fragile, but some lives are frighteningly strong. My elder daughter says that when you mow down weeds with a tractor, the weeds cling to the wheels of the tractor and spread seeds, to breed even at the moment they're being cut. Your baby latched on ferociously. He suckled so hard that I felt I would be sucked in, so I slapped the baby's bottom, which still had traces of redness from his birth. When that didn't work, I had to force him off. A baby who's lost its mother as soon as it's born intuitively doesn't want to let go when it's near a nipple. I laid the baby down and turned to go, and you asked me what my name was. You were the first person since I got married to ask me my name. Suddenly shy, I ducked my head.

"Park So-nyo."

You laughed then. I don't know why I did what I did next, just that I wanted to get you to laugh one more time. Even though you didn't ask, I told you that my older sister's name was Tae-nyo, which means "big girl." Our names—Little Girl and Big Girl. You laughed again. Then you said that your name was Eun-gyu and your elder brother was Kum-gyu. That your father gave you names containing the words "silver" and "gold," with the hope that you would earn money and live well. That he called you Silver Coffer and your brother Gold Coffer. That, perhaps because of that, your brother, Gold Coffer, lived a tiny bit better than you, Silver Coffer. That time I laughed. You laughed, watching me laugh. Then or now, you look best when you're laughing. So don't frown like that in front of the doctor; smile. A smile doesn't cost you any money.

. . .

Until your baby was three weeks old, I went to your house once a day and let the baby suckle. Sometimes it was early morning, sometimes in the middle of the night. Could that have been a burden for you? That was all I did for you, but for thirty years after that, I went to you whenever I hit a difficult patch. I think I started to go to you after what happened to Kyun. Because I just wanted to die. Because I thought it would be better to die. Everyone else made things difficult for me; only you didn't ask me anything. You told me that any wound healed as time passed. That I shouldn't think about anything, just calmly do what I was supposed to do. If you hadn't been there I don't know what would have happened to me; I was out of my mind with grief. You were the one who buried my fourth child, the stillborn, in the hills. Now that I think about it, did you move to Komso because I was too much for you? You weren't someone who was meant to live on the coast or work as a fisherman. You were someone who tilled the earth and planted seeds. You were someone who didn't have land of his own, and so tilled someone else's. I should have realized, when you went to Komso, that you left because it was hard for you to put up with me. I see that I was a terrible person to you.

It must be that a first meeting is important. I am sure that, deep down, I always thought you owed me, and I showed it by doing whatever I wanted. Just as I found you after you stole my basin on your bicycle, I found you after you moved to Komso without telling me. You didn't fit in at Komso. You looked out of place and strange standing by the sea. I can still see the expression on your face at the salt fields by the ocean. I was never able to forget that expression, but now that I think of it, maybe your expression was saying, Did she manage to find me even here?

Komso became a place I couldn't forget because of you. I always came to look for you when something happened that I couldn't handle by myself, but when I recovered some peace of mind I forgot about you. I thought I forgot about you. When you saw me in Komso, the first thing you said to me was "What's wrong?" I'm only saying this now; when I went to see you then, it was the first time I'd gone just to see you, not because something had happened to me.

Except for that one time when you ran off to Komso, you always stayed in the same place until I stopped needing you. Thank you for staying in the same place. I might have been able to go on living because of that. I'm sorry for going to see you every time I felt unsettled, but not even letting you hold my hand. Even though I went to you, when it seemed like you were coming to me I acted unkindly. That wasn't very nice of me. I'm sorry, so sorry. At first it was because I felt awkward, then because I felt we shouldn't, and later it was because I was old. You were my sin and my happiness. I wanted to seem dignified in your eyes.

Sometimes I told you stories I said I'd read, but I didn't actually read them. I had asked my daughter, and told you about them. Once, I told you that there was a place called Santiago in a country named Spain. You kept asking, "Where did you say it was?"—finding it hard to memorize that name. I told you that there was a pilgrimage route there that took thirty-three days to walk. Chi-hon wanted to go there—that's why she told me about that place—but I told you about it as if I wanted to go there. And you said, "If you want to go so badly, let's go together one of these days." My heart sank when I heard you say that. I think it was after that day that I stopped coming to you. Truthfully, I don't know where that place is, and I don't want to go there.

Do you know what happens to all the things we did together in the past? When I asked my daughter this, although it was you I wanted to ask, my daughter said, "It's so strange to hear you say something like this, Mom," and asked, "Wouldn't they have seeped into the present, not disappeared?" What difficult words! Do you understand what that means? She says that all the things that have happened are actually in the present, that old things are all mixed in with current things, and current things mingle with future things, and future things are combined with old things; it's just that we can't feel it. But now I can't go on.

Do you think that things happening now are linked to things from the past and things in the future, it's just that we can't feel them? I don't know, could that be true? Sometimes when I look at my grandchildren I think that they were dropped down from somewhere out of the blue, and that they have nothing to do with me. Nothing to do with me at all.

Would it have seeped in somewhere, the fact that the bicycle I saw you on when we first met had been stolen, that before you saw me walking down the avenue with the basin of flour on my head, you had planned to sell that stolen bicycle for a strand of seaweed? Or the fact that you ended up not being able to sell the bicycle, so you went to put it back where you found it, but the owner caught you and you got into trouble? Did those events seep into a page of the past and bring us all the way here?

I know that, after I disappeared, you went out and searched for me. I know that you, a man who had never been to Seoul before, came to Seoul Station and went around on the subway, stopping people who looked like me. And that you went by my house many times, hoping to hear some news about me. That you wanted to meet my children and hear what happened. Is that what made you so sick?

Your name is Lee Eun-gyu. When the doctor asks your name again, don't say "Park So-nyo"; say "Lee Eun-gyu." I will let go of you now. You were my secret. You were in my life, someone whose presence would never be guessed by anyone who knew me. Even though nobody knew that you were in my life, you were the person who brought a raft at every rapid current and helped me cross that water safely. I was happy that you were there. I came to tell you that I was able to travel through my life because I could come to you when I was anxious, not when I was happy.

I'm going to go now.

———

The house is frozen solid.

Why did you lock the door? You should have left it open so the neighborhood children could come in and play. There's no hint of heat anywhere. It's like a block of ice. Nobody has swept the snow away, even though it's snowed so much. The yard is a dazzling white. Icicles are hanging everywhere possible. When the children were growing up, they would break off the icicles and have swordfights. I suppose nobody is looking in on this house because I'm not here. It's been a long time since anyone's stopped by. Your motorcycle is propped up in the shed. And it's frozen solid, too. I wish you would stop riding that motorcycle. Who rides a motorcycle at your age? Do you think you're still young? There goes my habitual nagging once more. Then again, you looked strapping on your motorcycle, not like a man from the country. When you were young and rode into town on the motorcycle, hair pomaded, wearing a leather jacket, everyone turned to look. I think there's a picture from that time somewhere . . . in the frame above the door of the master bedroom. . . . Oh, there it is. It was taken when you weren't yet thirty years old. Your face is filled with passion; that's not the case now.

I remember the first house we lived in before we rebuilt. I really loved that house. Although now that I've said "love," I don't think it was only love. We lived forty-odd years in that house that doesn't exist anymore. I was always in that house. Always. You were there and not there. I didn't hear from you, as if you would never come back, but then you would return. Maybe that's why. I can see the old house in front of me, as if it's illuminated. I remember everything. All the things that happened in that house. The things that happened in the years when the children were born, the way I waited for you and forgot about you and hated you and waited for you again. Now the house is left behind, by itself. There's nobody here, and only the white snow is guarding the yard.

A house is such a strange thing. Everything else gets more worn when people handle it, and sometimes you can feel a person's poison if you get too close to him, but that's not what happens to a house. Even a good house falls apart quickly when nobody stops by. A house is alive only when there are people living in it, brushing against it, staying in it. Look at this—one end of the roof has collapsed because of the snow. In the spring you'll have to call the person who fixes the roof. There's a sticker with the name and number of the roof people in the television cabinet in the living room, but I don't know if you know about it. If you call them they'll come and take care of it. You can't leave the house empty like this in the winter. Even if nobody is living here, you have to come by and turn the boiler on once in a while.

Did you go to Seoul? Are you looking for me there?

This room, where I put the books Chi-hon sent down when she went to Japan, is cold, too. The books look frozen solid. After she sent the books here, this became my favorite room in the house. When I could tell that my head was going to hurt, I came in here and lay down. At first it seemed like I would get better. I didn't want to tell you that I was in pain. Then, as soon as I opened my eyes, the pain rushed at me, and I couldn't even cook for you, but I didn't want you to see me as a patient. That made me lonely, many times. I would go into the room with the books and lie down. One day, holding my pounding head, I promised myself that I would read at least one book that she wrote before she came back from Japan. And I went to learn how to read, still holding my head. I couldn't continue. When I tried to learn to read, my condition quickly got worse. I was lonely because I couldn't tell you that I was trying to learn to read. It would have hurt my pride to say something like that. When I learned to read, I wanted to do one more thing, besides reading my daughter's book with my own eyes: to write a farewell letter to every person in the family, before I became like this.

The wind, it's blowing so hard. The wind is rolling the snow in the yard and shifting it around.

Summer nights, when we set out the brazier and made steamed buns, were the best times we had in this yard. Hyong-chol would collect compost and make a fire to protect us from mosquitoes, and the younger ones would flop onto the platform and wait for the steamed buns to finish cooking in the pot on the brazier. When I made a whole pot of buns and set them out on a wicker tray, hands would shoot out, and the buns would all be gone. It took less time for the children to eat them than for me to steam them. As I put kindling in the brazier, I would look at the children lying on the platform together, waiting for another batch of buns, and it frightened me a little. How they could eat! Even though the fire was lit, the mosquitoes stuck incessantly to my arms and thighs and sucked my blood, and as the night became darker, the children ate all the buns and waited for more, while I kept steaming them. There were summer nights when, one by one, they fell asleep stretched over one another, waiting for the buns to cook. While they were sleeping, I would finish steaming the rest of the buns, put them in a basket, cover it, leave it on the platform, and go to sleep; the dawn dew slightly hardened the outside of the steamed buns. As soon as they woke up, the children would pull the basket toward them and eat some more. That's why my children still like cold steamed buns, the outsides slightly hardened. There were summer nights like that. Summer nights with stars pouring down from the sky.

When I was wandering the streets, I couldn't remember anything and my head was fuzzy, but I missed this place a lot. You don't know how much I missed it here, this yard, under the porch, the flower garden, the well. After wandering a while, I sat down on a street and drew in the dirt what came to mind. And it was the house. I drew the gate, I drew the flower garden, I drew the ledge of clay jars, I drew the porch. I couldn't remember anything except that house, the house that was here long before this house, that house that had disappeared a long time ago, that house with the traditional kitchen and the back yard shaded by butterbur leaves and the shed next to the pigsty. Those blue galvanized iron gates, their paint peeling. The gates of that house, with a smaller gate inset in the left one, and the mailbox to its right. There were only a few times that both gates needed to be opened, but the smaller inset gate, with a wooden handle, was always open to the alley. We never locked our doors. Even if we weren't at home, the neighborhood children came in through the inset gate and played until the sun set. During the busy farming season, my young daughter would come home from school, climb on the bicycle on its stand under the persimmon tree in the yard emptied of people, and pedal. When I came home, she would be sitting on the edge of the porch and jump into my arms, shouting, "Mom!" When my second son ran away from home, I left food out for him in the warmest part of the room and kept both big doors of the gate wide open. When someone tripped over the rice bowl and caused it to spill, I righted it. If I woke up in the middle of the night because of the wind, I would go outside and prop the doors open with heavy rocks, in case the wind closed them. My eyes and ears were trained on the gate, every time it made a noise.

The wardrobe is frozen solid, too.

The doors don't even open. But it should be empty. When my head started to hurt so badly, I wanted to go to that man, whom I hadn't seen in a long time. I thought maybe I would get better if I did. But I didn't go. I pressed down my desire to go, and went through my things. I could feel that it was approaching, the day when I wouldn't be able to recognize anything because I would be numb. I wanted to take care of all my things while I could still recognize them. I wrapped in a cloth the clothes I didn't wear, which I'd hung in the wardrobe, unable to throw them out, and burned them in the fields. The underclothes that Hyong-chol bought me with his first paycheck had been in the wardrobe for decades, with the tags still on. When I was burning them, my head felt like it would split in half. I burned everything I could, except the blankets and pillows, which the children could use when they came home for the holidays. I burned the cotton blankets that my

mother had made for me when I got married. I took out everything I'd spent a long time with and looked at it all again. The
things I never used because I was saving them, the dishes I collected to give my elder daughter when she got married. If I'd
known that she wasn't going to get married, even though her
younger sister is married and has three children, I would have
given them to my younger daughter. I stupidly thought I had
to give them to Chi-hon because I'd planned to give them to
her. I hesitated, then took them outside and smashed them
to pieces. I knew—one day I wouldn't remember anything.
And before that happened, I wanted to take care of everything
I'd ever used. I didn't want to leave anything behind. All the
bottom cupboards are empty, too. I broke everything that was
breakable and buried it all.

Even in that frozen wardrobe, the only winter clothing
would be the black mink coat my younger daughter bought
me. The year I turned fifty-five, I didn't want to eat or go out.
I spent my days buried deep in unpleasantness, feeling like my
face was being torn off. When I opened my mouth, I thought I
smelled something bad. At one point, I didn't say a word for
over ten days. I tried to shoo away negative thoughts, but
every day a sad thought was added to my collection. Even
though it was in the middle of winter, I kept dipping my hands
in cold water and washing and washing them. And one day I
went to church. I stopped in the churchyard. I bent over the
feet of the Holy Mother, who was holding her dead son, to
pray for her help to pull me out of this depression, which I
couldn't stand any longer, to beg her to take pity on me. But
then I stopped myself, wondering what more I could ask of

someone holding her dead son. During mass, I saw that the woman in front of me was wearing a black mink coat. Drawn by its softness, I quietly lowered my face to it, without even realizing I was doing it. The mink, like a spring breeze, gently embraced my old face. The tears I'd been holding back poured out. The woman moved away when I kept trying to rest my head on her mink coat. When I got home, I called my younger daughter and asked her to buy me a mink coat. It was the first time I'd opened my mouth in ten days.

"A mink coat, Mom?"

"Yes, a mink coat."

She was quiet.

"Are you going to buy me one or not?"

"It's not that cold this year. Do you have someplace to wear a mink coat to?"

"Yes."

"Are you going somewhere?"

"No."

She laughed out loud at my curt replies. "Come to Seoul, then. We can go shopping together."

As we walked into the department store, to the mink coats, my daughter kept looking at me without saying anything. I had no idea that my mink coat, which was slightly shorter than the one I had buried my face in, the one that woman in church was wearing, was such an expensive thing. My daughter didn't tell me. When we went home with the mink coat, my daughter-in-law's eyes bulged. "A mink coat, Mother!"

I was quiet.

"You're so lucky, Mother. To have a daughter who buys

you expensive things like this. I haven't even been able to buy my mother a fox scarf. They say a mink gets handed down for generations. When you pass away, you should leave it to me."

"It's the first time Mom ever asked me to buy something for her! Stop it!"

When my daughter shot back at her sister-in-law as if she was angry, I realized it. The reason she kept looking at the price tag, again and again. And the reason she kept looking at me. At that time, she had just graduated from college and was working at a hospital pharmacy. When I got back from Seoul, I took the mink coat and went to a similar store in town and asked the girl working in the mink-coat department how much it cost. I froze. Who knew one piece of clothing could cost so much! I called my daughter to tell her that we should return the coat, and she told me, "Mom, you have every right to wear that coat. You should wear it."

In this region, there are very few cold days in winter, so I could wear a mink coat only occasionally. Once, I didn't wear it for three years. When I had depressed thoughts, I opened the wardrobe and buried my face in the mink coat. And I thought, When I die, I will leave it to my younger daughter.

Although it's frozen now, in the spring the flower garden near the wall will come alive again. The blossoms on the neighbor's pear tree will bloom, and their scent will float over. The rose vines with pale-pink buds will flex their spikes, cheering. The weeds under the wall will grow thick and tall with the first spring rain. Once, I bought thirty ducklings from under the bridge in town and let them out in the yard, and they rushed over to the flower garden and stepped on all the flowers. When they ran around in packs with the chicks, it was hard to tell which were ducklings and which were chicks. Anyway, in the spring, the yard was noisy because of them. It was in this yard that my daughter, who was digging under the rosebush, saying that it would yield a lot of flowers if it was given manure, saw a wriggling worm in the dirt, threw the short hoe aside, and ran inside; the hoe hit a chick and killed it. I remember the wave of the smell of dirt that would reach my nose when, in the summer, a sudden rain fell, and the dog and chickens and ducks that had been wandering around the yard crawled under the porch and into the chicken cages and under the wall. I remember the droplets of dirt formed by the sudden rain. On windy late-fall nights, the leaves of the persimmon tree in the side yard would rustle off and fly around. All night, we would hear them scuttling across the yard. During snowy winter nights, the wind would blow the snow piled in the yard onto the porch.

Someone is opening the gate. Ah, Aunt!

You were an aunt to my children and a sister to me, but I was never able to call you "sister": you seemed more like my mother-in-law. I see you have come to check on the house, because it's snowing and windy. I thought nobody was here to look after this house, forgetting that you're here. But why are you limping? You're always so spry. I guess you're getting old, too. Be careful—it's snowy.

"Anyone home?"

Your voice is still powerful, like it's always been.

"Nobody's here, right?"

You are calling out even though you know nobody is here. You sit on the edge of the porch, not waiting for an answer. Why did you come without wearing enough layers? You'll catch a cold. You're looking at the snow in the yard as if you're somewhere else. What are you thinking?

"It feels like someone's here. . . ."

Halfway to being a ghost, Aunt.

"I don't know where you're wandering around when it's this cold."

Are you talking about me?

"The summer went by, and fall went by, and it's winter. . . . I didn't know you were such a heartless person. What is this house going to do without you? It's just an empty shell. You left wearing summer clothes, and you haven't come back even though it's winter—are you already someone of the other world?"

Not yet. I'm wandering around like this.

"The saddest person in the world is the one who dies outside their home. . . . Please be alert and come back home."

Are you crying?

Your eyes, long slants, look up at the gray sky and become wet. Your eyes aren't scary at all, now that you're acting like this. I was always so frightened by your stern eyes that I honestly didn't look at your face, so as not to meet your eyes. But I think I liked you better when you were no-nonsense. This doesn't seem like you, sitting with your shoulders drooping. I was never able to hear anything nice from you when I was alive, so why do I have to look at your dejected figure now? I don't like seeing you weak. I wasn't only afraid of you. If something difficult happened and I didn't know what to do, I thought, What would Aunt do? And I would choose what I thought you would do. So you were my role model, too. You know I have a temper. All the relationships in the world are two-way, not determined by one side. And now you're going to have to look after Hyong-chol's father, who's all alone. I don't feel good about it, either. But since you are near him, I feel a little better. When I was alive, I knew full well that you were depending on Hyong-chol's father, since you were all alone, and I didn't feel hurt or left out or disappointed. I just thought of you as a difficult elder of the family. So much so that you felt like our mother and not our sister. But, Aunt . . . I don't want to go to the grave set aside for me a few years ago at the ancestral grave site. I don't want to go there. When I lived here and woke up from the fog in my head, I would walk by myself to the grave site set aside for me, so that I could feel comfortable if I lived there after death. It was sunny, and I liked the pine tree that stood bent but tall, but remaining a member of this family even in death would be too much and too hard. To try to change my mind, I would sing and pull weeds, sitting there until the sun set, but nothing made me feel comfortable there. I lived with this family for over fifty years; please let me go now. Back then, when we were assigning grave sites and you said my plot should go on a site down the slope from yours, I glared and said, "Oh, so even when I'm dead I can do your errands." I remember saying that. Don't be upset about it, Aunt. I thought about it a long time, but I didn't say that with ill will. I just want to go home. I'll go rest there.

. . .

Oh, I see the shed door is open.

The wind is pounding at the shed door as if it would knock it down. There's a thin layer of ice on the wooden platform that I liked to sit on. If someone sat there without seeing the ice, he would slip right off. Chi-hon used to read in this shed. Getting bitten by fleas. I knew that she crept in here with a book, in between the pigsty and the ash shed. I didn't look for her. When Hyong-chol asked where she was, I said I didn't know. Because I liked seeing her read. Because I didn't want to disturb her. Straw was piled on the board covering the pigsty. Chickens would have taken over one side and would be laying and sitting on eggs. Nobody would find the child squeezed in there, on top of the straw pile, putting spit on her flea bites to soothe them, reading. How much fun must it have been for her to hide there, reading, hearing her brother opening doors, pushing into the kitchen, looking for her? And the chickens, how particular were they? Huddled over eggs on the straw pile on top of the pigsty, they would get annoyed at the sound of my daughter turning pages. These chickens, who didn't lay eggs if we didn't make their nests cozy and tempting with nest eggs, became sensitive to Chi-hon's rustling, and one time they cackled so much that her brother found her. What did she read, hidden quietly in the shed, with a pig grunting next to her and the chickens clucking above her and the hoe and rake and shovel and all kinds of farm equipment and straw around her?

In the spring, the dog, growling, would lie with her new litter under the porch, where the family's winter shoes were scattered. You could hear the water dripping from the eaves.

That gentle dog, why did she get so aggressive when she had pups? Unless you were a member of the family, you couldn't get near her. When she had a litter, Hyong-chol would repaint the sign on the blue gate that always hung there, the one that said "Beware of Dog." Once, I took a puppy from the porch while the dog was sleeping after her dinner, put it in a basket, covered it with a cloth, and, with my hand, covered where I thought the eyes were, and brought it to Aunt's.

"Why are you covering its eyes when it's so dark out, Mom?" asked my younger daughter, following me. She looked confused, even after I explained that if I didn't do it the pup would find its way home.

"Even though it's so dark?"

"Yes, even though it's this dark!"

When the dog discovered that her puppy was gone, she refused to eat, and lay around, sick. She had to eat to make enough milk to feed the other puppies, so they could grow. It looked like she would die if I left her alone, so I brought the pup back and pushed it next to her, and the dog started eating again. That dog lived under that porch.

Oh, I don't know where to stop these memories, the memories that are sprouting all over the place like spring greens. Everything I forgot about is rushing back. From the rice bowls on the kitchen shelf to the big and little clay jars on the condiment ledge, from the narrow wooden stairs to the attic to the pumpkin vines spreading thick under the dirt wall, climbing up.

. . .

You shouldn't leave the house to freeze like this.

If it's too much, ask our younger daughter-in-law for help. She always carefully looked after their house, even though it wasn't their own. She has an eye for this kind of thing, and she's exact and warm. Even though she works, her house is always sparkling clean, and she doesn't even have help. If it's hard to maintain the house, try talking to her. I'm telling you, if she touches an old thing it becomes new. Don't you remember how they rented, in the redevelopment area, a brick house that the owner didn't maintain, and she mixed cement with her own hands and fixed it? A house takes on the characteristics of its occupant, and, depending on who lives in it, it can become a very good house or a very strange house. When spring comes, please plant some flowers in the yard, and rub down the floors, and fix the roof that collapsed from the snow.

A few years ago, when someone asked you while you were drunk where you lived, you said Yokchon-dong. Even though it's been twenty years since Hyong-chol left Yokchon-dong. Even though Yokchon-dong has become faint even in my memory. You never really showed happiness or sadness. When Hyong-chol bought his first house, in Yokchon-dong, in Seoul, you didn't say much, but in your heart I suppose you were very proud. And that's why, when you were drunk, you forgot about this house and you named that house, where we would go three or four times a year, like guests, and stay one or sometimes two nights. I wish you would think about this house in that way. Around this house, small flowers bloomed every year and lived prettily until they faded, in the corner of the yard or near the back yard, without my having to plant them. In the yard and under the porch and in the back yard, something was always gathering or coming or going or dying. Birds landed on the clothesline as if they were talking laundry, and they played and chattered and twittered. I do think that a house starts resembling the people who live there. Otherwise, would the ducks living in that house have roamed around the yard and laid eggs anywhere? Otherwise, would I remember so clearly how, on a sunny day, I would sweep thinly sliced dried radish or boiled taro stems into a wicker tray and perch it on top of the dirt wall? Would the image of my daughter's newly washed, clean white sneakers drying under the sunlight hover like this? Chi-hon liked to look at the sky reflected in the well over there. I can almost see her interrupting herself as she drew water from the well, looking down with her chin in her hands.

Be well. . . . I'm leaving this house now.

———

Last summer, when I was left behind at Seoul Station, I could only remember things from when I was three years old. Having forgotten everything, I could do nothing but walk— I didn't even know who I was. I walked and walked. Everything was foggy. The yard I used to play in when I was three came clearly to me. That was when my father, who dug for gold and coal, came home. I walked as far as I could go. In between apartment buildings, along grassy hills and soccer fields, I walked and walked. Where did I want to go, walking like that? Could it be the yard I played in as a three-year-old? When Father came home, he went to work every morning at the construction site for a new train station that was ten ri away. What was the accident he had? What kind of accident was it that cost him his life? They say that when neighbors came to tell Mom about Father's accident, I was running around the yard. I played, watching Mom staggering, her face turning ashen, supported by neighbors, going to the accident site. Someone passing by said, "Here you are laughing, not even knowing that your father died, you silly child," and smacked my bottom. With only that memory, I walked and walked until I collapsed from exhaustion.

———

Over there.

Mom is sitting on the porch of the dim house I was born in.

Mom raises her head and looks at me. My grandmother had a dream when I was being born. A cow with a shiny brown coat was stretching, having just woken, raising its knees. My grandmother said I would be very energetic, since I was born just as the cow was using its energy to get up, and said that I should be well taken care of, because I would become the source of a lot of joy. Mom looks at my foot, the strap of the blue plastic sandal digging into it. The bone is visible through the wound in my foot. Mom's face crumples in sorrow. That face is the face I saw when I looked into the mirror of the wardrobe after I gave birth to a dead baby. "My baby," Mom says, and opens her arms. Mom puts her hands under my armpits as if she's holding a child who has just died. She takes the blue plastic sandals off my feet and pulls my feet into her lap. Mom doesn't smile. She doesn't cry. Did Mom know? That I, too, needed her my entire life?

Rosewood Rosary

IT'S BEEN NINE MONTHS since Mom went missing.

You're in Italy now. Sitting on the marble stairs overlooking St. Peter's Square in Vatican City, you're looking at the obelisk from Egypt. The guide, sweat beaded on his forehead, shouts, "Come this way," and directs people in your tour group to the bottom of the stairs, where there is shade, near the large pinecones. "We are not allowed to speak in the museums or the basilica, so I'll tell you about the important things in the museum before we go in. I'll distribute earphones, so please listen."

You take the earphones, but you don't put them in your ears. The guide continues: "If you don't hear anything in the earphones, it means you're too far away from me. There will be so many people that I won't be able to look out for each and every one of you. I can guide you properly only when you're near me, where you can hear my voice."

You head for the bathroom with the earphones dangling around your neck. People in your group stare at you as you stride into the bathroom. You wash your hands at the sink, and when you open your purse to take out your handkerchief to wipe your hands, your gaze stops at your sister's letter crumpled inside. It's the letter you took out of your mailbox at your apartment three days ago, as you were leaving Seoul with Yu-bin. Holding your suitcase in one hand, standing outside your door, you read your sister's name written on the envelope. It was the first time you'd received a letter from your sister. And it was a handwritten letter, not just an e-mail. You wondered if you should open it, but you just stuffed it into your purse. Perhaps you thought that if you read it you would not be able to get on the plane with Yu-bin.

You come out of the bathroom and sit down with the group. Instead of putting the earphones in your ears, however, you take out your sister's letter, hold it for a moment, then rip the envelope open.

Sister.

When I went to Mom's soon after coming back from America, she gave me a young persimmon tree that came up to my knees. It was when I went to get the things I'd left there. Mom was crumpled in the storage area next to the shed, where my cooktop stove and fridge and table were stored. She was lying there, her limbs limp. The neighborhood cats that Mom fed were sitting around her. When I shook her, she managed to open her eyes, as if she were waking up, and looked at me and smiled. She said, "You're here, my baby daughter!" Mom told me she was fine. Now I see that she had lost consciousness, but she insisted that she was fine, that she was in the storage shed to feed the cats. Mom had kept everything I left there when I went to America. Even the rubber gloves I told her to use as I was leaving. She said that she almost used the portable gas range during one ancestral rite but then didn't. "Why not?" I asked, and she said, "So I could give everything back to you the way you left it when you came home."

When I finished loading all the things onto the truck, Mom came over with the persimmon tree from behind the house, where she kept all the condiment jars. She looked embarrassed. The roots of the tree were wrapped in dirt and plastic. She had bought it for the yard at our new place. It was so small that I wondered when it would start bearing fruit. Honestly, I didn't want to bring it back. We were going to live in a house with a yard, but we didn't own it, and I wondered who would take care of the tree. Mom, seeing through me, said, "You'll find persimmons on this tree very soon; even seventy years go by quick."

I still didn't want to take it, but Mom said, "It's so when I die you can pick persimmons and think about me."

Mom started saying "When I die . . ." more frequently. You know, that was her weapon for a long time. Her only weapon when it came to kids who didn't do things the way she wanted them to. I don't know when it started, but when she didn't approve of something, Mom would say, "Do that after I die." I brought the little persimmon tree to Seoul on the truck, although I didn't know if it would survive, and buried the roots in the ground, as deep as Mom had marked on the tree. Later, when Mom came to Seoul, she said I'd planted it too close to the wall and that I should move it to another spot. She asked me often if I'd moved it. I said yes, even though I hadn't. Mom wanted me to move the tree to an empty spot in the yard where I thought I could plant a big tree if I had enough money to buy this house. I didn't really think I would move the little tree, which only had a couple of branches and now barely came up to my waist, but I answered yes. Before she went missing, she suddenly started calling every other day, asking, "Did you move the persimmon tree?" I just said, "I'll do it later."

Sister. Not until yesterday, with the baby on my back, did I take a cab to So-orung and buy powdered chicken droppings, dig a hole on the spot Mom had pointed out, and move the persimmon tree there. I hadn't felt at all bad when I didn't listen to her and failed to move that tiny persimmon tree away from the wall, but now I was surprised. When I first brought the tree here, the roots were so scrawny that I kept looking at it, doubting that it could even grow in the ground, but when I dug it up to move it, its roots had already spread far underground, tangled. I was impressed with its grit for life, its determination to survive somehow in the barren earth. Did she mean to give me the tree so that I could watch its branches multiply and its trunk thicken? Was it to tell me that if I wanted to see fruit I had to take good care of it? Or maybe she just didn't have money to buy a big tree. For the first time, I felt attached to that persimmon tree. My doubts that it could ever have fruit disappeared.

Do you remember asking me a while ago to tell you something that only I knew about Mom? I told you I didn't know Mom. All I knew was that Mom was missing. It's the same now. I especially don't know where her strength came from. Think about it. Mom did things that one person couldn't do by herself. I think that's why she became emptier and emptier. Finally, she became someone who couldn't find any of her kids' houses. I don't recognize myself, feeding my kids and brushing *their hair and sending them to school, unable to go look for Mom even though she's missing. You said I was different, unlike other young moms these days, that there was a small part of me that's a little bit like her, but, sister, no matter what, I don't think I can be like Mom. Since she went missing, I often think: Was I a good daughter? Could I do the kind of things for my kids she did for me?*

I know one thing. I can't do it like she did. Even if I wanted to. When I'm feeding my kids, I often feel annoyed, burdened, as if they're holding on to my ankles. I love my kids, and I am moved— wondering, did I really give birth to them? But I can't give them my entire life like Mom did. Depending on the situation, I act as if I would give them my eyes if they need them, but I'm not Mom. I keep wishing the baby would hurry and grow up. I feel that my life has stalled because of the kids. Once the baby's a little older, I'm going to send him to day care, or find someone to sit with him, and go to work. That's what I'm going to do. Because I have my life, too. When I realized this about myself, I wondered how Mom did it the way she did, and discovered that I didn't really know her. Even if we say her situation made her think only about us, how could we have thought of Mom as Mom her entire life? Even though I'm a mother, I have so many dreams of my own, and I remember things from my childhood, from when I was a girl and a young woman, and I haven't forgotten a thing. So why did we think of Mom as a mom from the very beginning? She didn't have the opportunity to pursue her dreams and, all by herself, faced everything the era dealt her, poverty and sadness, and she couldn't do anything about her very bad lot in life other than suffer through it and get beyond it and live her life to the very best of her ability, giving her body and her heart to it completely. Why did I never give a thought to Mom's dreams?

Sister.

I wanted to shove my face into the hole I dug for the persimmon tree. If I can't live like Mom, how could she have wanted to live like that? Why did this thought never occur to me when she was with us? Even though I'm her daughter, I had no idea, so how alone must she have felt with other people? How unfair is it that all she did was sacrifice everything for us, and she wasn't understood by anyone?

Sister. Do you think we'll be able to be with her again, even if it's just for one day? Do you think I'll be given the time to understand Mom and hear her stories and console her for her old dreams that are buried somewhere in the pages of time? If I'm given even a few hours, I'm going to tell her that I love all the things she did, that I love Mom, who was able to do all of that, that I love Mom's life, which nobody remembers. That I respect her.

Sister, please don't give up on Mom, please find Mom.

Your sister must not have been able to write the date or a goodbye. The letter has round blotches on it, as if she'd been crying as she wrote it. Your eyes linger over the yellowed spots; then you fold the letter and put it back in your purse. As your sister was writing the letter, her youngest, who had probably been eating something off the floor under the table, may have come to her and clumsily started to sing the children's song that starts, "Mommy Bear . . . ," hanging on to her. Your sister may have looked at her baby, although with a dark expression, and sung for him, ". . . is slim!" The baby, who would not have understood his mom's emotions, may have grinned broadly, and said "Daddy Bear . . . ," waiting for your sister to finish the verse. Your sister may have finished it, "is fat!" Your sister may not have been able to write the end to her letter. The baby, trying to climb up your sister's leg, may have fallen down, bumping his head on the floor. And the baby would have burst into desperate-sounding sobs. Your sister, seeing the bluish bruise spreading on the baby's soft skin, may have then spilled the tears she had been holding back.

You fold the letter and put it in your purse, and the guide's passionate voice echoes in your ears. "The highlight of this museum is the *Creation of Adam,* on the ceiling of the Sistine Chapel, which we will see at the end. Michelangelo hung from a beam on the ceiling for four years as he worked on the fresco, and later in life, his eyesight became so weak that he couldn't read or see pictures unless he went outside. Frescoes are made with lime plaster, so they had to finish before the plaster set. If they couldn't do the work, which would normally take about a month, in one day, the plaster set and they had to do it again. Because he had to hang from the ceiling like that for four years, it's understandable that he had problems with his neck and back for the rest of his life."

The last thing you did at the airport before you boarded the plane was to call your father. After Mom disappeared, your father went back and forth between his house and Seoul, but he went home for good in the spring. You called him every day, in the morning or sometimes at night. Father picked up the phone after one ring, as if he was waiting by it. He would say your name before you told him it was you. This was something Mom always did. She would be pulling weeds in the flower garden, and when the phone rang, she would say to

Father, "Answer the phone, it's Chi-hon!" When you asked how she could tell who was calling, Mom shrugged and would say, "I just . . . I just know." Living in the empty house by himself, without Mom, Father could now tell it was you, from the first ring. You told Father that you might not be able to call for a while, since you would have to think about when he would be awake to call from Rome. Father suddenly said, as if he wasn't listening to you carefully, that he should have let Mom get surgery for sinus empyema.

"Mom had pain in her nose, too?" you asked, your voice dull, and Father said that Mom couldn't sleep when the seasons changed because she would be coughing. He said, "It's my fault. It was because of me that your mom didn't have time to look after herself." On any other day, you would have said, "Father, it's nobody's fault," but on that day, the words "Yes, it's your fault" jumped out of your mouth. Father drew in his breath sharply on the other end of the phone. He didn't know you were calling from the airport.

"Chi-hon," Father said after a long pause.

"Yes."

"Your mom isn't even in my dreams anymore."

You didn't say anything.

Father was quiet for a moment, then started speaking of the old days. He said that one day they cooked a scabbard fish that Hyong-chol had sent down. Mom dug up a radish topped with green leaves from the hillside garden, brushed off the dirt, peeled it with a knife, cut it into big chunks, spread it on the bottom of a pot, and steamed the scabbard fish, which turned red from all the seasonings she added. Mom plucked a plump piece of fish and set it on Father's bowl of rice. Father wept as he recalled that one spring day, when they shared for lunch the scabbard fish that Mom had cooked in the morning and, stomachs full, napped together, stretched out. He said that back then he didn't know that this was happiness. "I feel bad for your mom. I complained I was sick all the time." It was true. Father was either away from home or, when he was home, sick. He seemed to be remorseful about that now.

"When I started getting sick, the same thing must have been happening to your mom."

Was Mom unable to say that she was in pain, pushed aside by Father's illnesses? Because she took care of everyone in the family, Mom was someone who couldn't be sick. When he turned fifty, Father started taking blood-pressure medication, and his joints ached, and he developed cataracts. Right before Mom went missing, Father had a series of surgical procedures done on his knee, over a year, and because it was difficult for him to urinate, he had an operation on his prostate. He collapsed from a stroke and went to the hospital three times in one year, and each time he was released fifteen days or a month later, and the cycle was repeated. Every time this happened, Mom slept at the hospital. The family hired an aide for Father, but at night Mom had to sleep there. On the first night the aide slept over at the hospital, Father went into the bathroom, locked the door, and refused to come out. Mom, who was staying with Hyong-chol, got a phone call from the aide, who didn't know what to do about Father's sudden rebellion. Mom went to the hospital at once, even though it was in the middle of the night, and soothed Father, who was still locked inside the bathroom.

"It's me. Open the door, it's me."

Father, who had refused to open the door no matter what anyone said, opened the door when he heard Mom's voice. He was crouching next to the toilet. Mom helped him out to his bed; Father gazed at her for a while and finally fell asleep. He said he didn't remember any of this. The next day, you asked him why he had done that, and he asked you, "You mean I did that?" And, worried you would continue to question him, he quickly closed his eyes.

"Mom has to rest, too, Father."

Father had turned away. You knew that he was pretending to sleep but listening to you and Mom. Mom said she thought he had done it because he was afraid. He woke up, and he wasn't at home but at the hospital, where there were only strangers and no family, and he must have hidden himself, wondering where he was, frightened.

"What's so scary about this?" your father must have heard you muttering.

"Haven't you ever been scared?" Mom glanced at Father and continued in a low voice: "Your father says that I do that sometimes, too. He says when he wakes up in the middle of the night and I'm not there and he looks for me, I'm hiding in the shed, or behind the well, waving my hands in front of me, and saying, 'Don't do that to me.' He says he finds me shivering."

"You, Mom?"

"I don't remember doing that. Your father says he had to take me in and lay me down and give me some water, and finally I'd fall asleep. If I'm like that, I'm sure your Father's afraid, too."

"Afraid of what?"

Mom mumbled faintly, "I think it was scary just to live day by day. The scariest thing was when there was nothing left in the rice jar. When I thought I had to let you children go hungry . . . my lips were dry with dread. There were days like that."

Father never told you or anyone else in the family that Mom acted that way sometimes. When you called him after Mom went missing, he brought up random old stories to delay the end of your conversation, but he never told you that Mom had gone to hide somewhere in the middle of the night, while she was sleeping.

———

You look at your watch. It's ten in the morning. Is Yu-bin up? Has he had breakfast?

Today you woke up at six in the morning in an old hotel facing Termini Station. After Mom went missing, a heavy despair weighed down your body and your heart, as if you were sinking in water. You made to rise from the bed, and Yu-bin, who was sleeping with his back to you, turned around and tried to embrace you. You took his arm and rested it gently on the bed. Rejected, he put his arm on his forehead and said, "You should sleep a little more."

"I can't sleep."

He moved his arm and turned over. You gazed at his stubborn back, then reached out and stroked it—your boyfriend's back, which you haven't been able to embrace warmly since Mom went missing.

Your family, who were all exhausted from looking for Mom, would often sink into silence when you were together. And then you would all act out. One of you would kick the door open to leave, or pour soju into a large beer mug and gulp it down. Pushing away the memories of Mom that were sprouting up all around you, you all thought one thing: If only Mom were here. If only Mom would say one more time from the other end of the phone, "It's me!" Mom always said, "It's me!" After she went missing, your family couldn't maintain any sort of conversation for more than ten minutes. The question *Where is Mom now?* trickled in between whatever thoughts you had, making you anxious.

"I think I want to be by myself today," you ventured.

"What are you going to do by yourself?" he asked, still facing the other way.

"I want to go to St. Peter's Basilica. Yesterday, while I was waiting for you in the lobby, I signed up for the Vatican tour. I have to get ready and go. They said we were leaving at seven-twenty from the lobby. They said that the line gets so long that if we don't get there by nine, it will take more than two hours to get inside."

"You can go with me tomorrow."

"We're in Rome. There are so many other places I can go with you."

You washed your face quietly, so as to not disturb him. You wanted to wash your hair, but you thought the sound of the water would be too loud, so you just tied your hair back, looking at your reflection in the mirror. When you emerged from the bathroom after getting dressed, you said, as if you just remembered, "Thanks for bringing me here."

He pulled the sheet over his face. You knew that he was being as patient as he could possibly be. He introduced you as his wife to people you met here. You would probably be his wife by now, if Mom had been found. After his morning seminar, you two were supposed to have lunch with a few other couples. If he went to lunch by himself, the others would ask him where his wife was. You glanced at your boyfriend, the sheet still pulled over his head, and left the room.

After your mom went missing, you developed impulsive behaviors. You drank impulsively, and you would impulsively take a train down to your parents' home in the country. You stared at the ceiling of your studio, unable to sleep, then got up and ran around the streets of Seoul, pasting flyers, whether it was in the middle of the night or at dawn. You once burst into the police station and screamed at them to find your mom. Hyong-chol came to the police station after receiving a call, and just stared at you. "Find Mom!" you screamed at your brother, who at a certain point had started to accept Mom's absence, sometimes even going golfing.

Your scream was both a protest against people who knew Mom and hatred for yourself, who hadn't been able to find her. Your brother calmly listened to your shrieking attacks: "How can you be like this? Why aren't you finding Mom? Why? Why!"

All your brother could do was to walk the city with you at night. You would search underground concourses, wearing the mink coat that you took from Mom's closet and brought with you last winter, or with the coat slung over your arm— so that you could drape it on Mom, who was last seen wearing summer clothes, when you found her. Your shadow holding the mink coat would be cast on the marble buildings as you walked among the sleeping homeless who were using newspaper or ramen crates as blankets. You kept your phone on all the time, but now nobody called to say they had seen someone who looked like Mom.

One day, you went to Seoul Station, to the spot where Mom was left behind, and bumped into your eldest brother, who was standing there aimlessly. You sat together, watching the subway trains come and go, until service ended for the night. He said that at first when he sat there like that he thought Mom would appear and tap him on the shoulder and say, "Hyong-chol!" But now he didn't think that was going to happen. He mentioned that he didn't think anymore, that the inside of his head was blank. That when he doesn't want to go home right away after work, he finds himself coming to the station.

One holiday, you went to his house. You saw your brother get out of the car with his golf clubs and screamed, "You asshole!" and made a scene. If even your brother accepts Mom's disappearance, who in the world is going to find her? You grabbed his clubs and threw them on the ground. Everyone was slowly becoming the son, daughter, and husband whose mom and wife was missing. Even without Mom, daily life continued.

Another time, you went back in the early morning to the spot where Mom had gone missing, and you again bumped into your brother. From behind, you grabbed him in a hug as he stood in the dawn light. He said that maybe it was only her children who thought of Mom's life as being filled with pain and sacrifice, because of our guilt. We might actually be diminishing her life as something useless. To his credit, he remembered something Mom always said, even when the smallest positive thing happened: "I'm thankful! It's something we should be grateful for!" Mom expressed gratitude for the small moments of happiness that everyone experienced. Your brother said that Mom's gratitude came from the heart, that she was thankful about everything, that someone who was so grateful couldn't have led an unhappy life. When you said goodbye, your brother said he was afraid that Mom wouldn't recognize him even if she came back. You told him that, for Mom, he was the most precious person in the world, that Mom would always recognize him, no matter where he was or how he changed. When he was drafted into the army and entered training camp, there was a day when parents were invited to visit. Mom made rice cakes and carried them on her head to see Hyong-chol, with you in tow. Even though hundreds of soldiers were wearing the same clothes and demonstrating the same taekwondo moves, she was able to pick out your brother. To you, they all looked the same, but Mom smiled a great big smile and pointed: "There's your brother!"

For once, you were peacefully talking about Mom with your brother, but then you raised your voice, asking why he wasn't doing more to look for her. "Why are you talking about Mom as if she won't be able to come back?" you yelled. He said, "Tell me, how am I supposed to find her?" In his frustration, he ripped open the top few buttons of his white shirt under his suit jacket, and ended up showing you his tears. After that, he stopped answering your calls.

Only after Mom went missing did you realize that her stories were piled inside you, in endless stacks. Mom's everyday life used to go on in a repeating loop, without a break. Her everyday words, which you didn't think deeply about and sometimes dismissed as useless when she was with you, awoke in your heart, creating tidal waves. You realized that her position in life hadn't changed even after the war was over, and even when the family could afford to feed itself. When the family got together for the first time in a long while, sat around the table with Father, and talked about the presidential elections, Mom would cook and bring out the food and wash the dishes and clean and hang damp dishrags to dry. Mom took care of fixing the gate and the roof and the porch. Instead of helping her do the work that she did nonstop, even you thought of it as natural, and took it for granted that this was her job. Sometimes, as your brother pointed out, you thought of her life as disappointing—even though Mom, despite never having been well off, tried so hard to give you the best of everything, even though it was Mom who patted your back soothingly when you were lonely.

Around the time tiny new leaves started to sprout on the ginkgo trees in front of City Hall, you were squatting under a large tree on a main road that led to Samchong-dong. It was unbelievable that spring was coming without Mom here. That the frozen ground was thawing and the trees were starting to wake up. Your heart, which had sustained you throughout this ordeal with the belief that you would be able to find Mom, was crushed. *Even though Mom's missing, summer will come and fall will come again and winter will come, like this. And I'll be living in a world without Mom.* You could imagine a desolate road. And the missing woman plodding down that road, wearing blue plastic sandals.

Without telling anyone in the family, you left with Yu-bin for Rome, where he was going to attend a seminar. He'd asked you to come with him but didn't expect you to say yes. When you actually decided to go with him, he was a little taken aback, though he patiently made a few changes in his schedule. The day before you were to leave, he even called to ask, "Nothing's changed, right?" As you got on the Rome-bound plane with him, you wondered for the first time whether Mom's dream was to travel. Mom would always worry and tell you

not to get on planes, but when you came back from somewhere, she would ask you detailed questions about the place
you'd visited: "What kind of clothes do Chinese people
wear?" "How do the Indians carry their children?" "What
was the most delicious food you had in Japan?" Mom's questions would spill out onto you. You would always reply
curtly, "Chinese men take off their shirts in the summer and
walk around like that." "The Indian woman I saw in Peru carried her child wrapped in a sack on her hip." "Japanese food
is too sweet." When Mom asked more questions, you got
annoyed and said, "I'll tell you later, Mom!" But you had no
opportunity for these conversations later, because you always
had something else to do. You leaned back in your airplane
seat and heaved a deep sigh. It was Mom who'd told you to live
someplace far away. It was also Mom who'd sent you at a
young age to live in a city far from your birthplace. Mom back
in those days—you realized, painfully, that Mom was the same
age as you are now when she brought you to the city and left,
taking the night train back home. One woman. That woman
disappeared, bit by bit, having forgotten the joy of being born
and her childhood and dreams, marrying before her first
period and having five children and raising them. The woman
who, at least when it came to her children, wasn't surprised or
thrown off by anything. The woman whose life was marred
with sacrifice until the day she went missing. You compare
yourself with Mom, but Mom was an entire world unto herself. If you were Mom, you wouldn't be running away like
this, running away from fear.

.   .   .

The entire city of Rome is literally a historical site. All the negative things you heard about Rome—there's a transit strike every other day, and they don't even apologize to the passengers; people will grab your arm and steal your watch right under your nose; the streets are blighted with graffiti and garbage—you didn't care about. You just observed everything passively, although you were ripped off by a cab driver, and someone grabbed the sunglasses that you had just placed next to you at a café. You went to various ruins by yourself, during the three days when Yu-bin was at his conference. To the Foro Romano, the Colosseum, the Baths of Caracalla, the Catacombs. You stood listlessly in the spacious ruins of the large city. Everything about Rome symbolized civilization. But although traces of the past were spread out in front of you wherever you went, you didn't keep anything in your heart.

Now you are looking at the statues of saints in the round piazza, but your eyes do not pause anywhere. The guide explains that Vatican City is not only a country in the secular world, but also God's country; that the territory is only forty-four hectares but an independent state with its own currency and stamps. You aren't listening to the guide's explanations. Your eyes jump from person to person. Even if there are only a few people around, your eyes leap among them, unsettled, as you wonder, Is Mom here somewhere? There's no way Mom would be among Western tourists, but even now your eyes don't know how to settle on a single object. Your eyes meet the eyes of the guide, who'd said that he came here seven years ago to study choral music. Embarrassed that you're not even wearing the earphones, you pull them up and plug them into your ears. "Vatican City is the world's smallest country. But thirty thousand people visit it in a single day." As you hear the guide's commentary transmitted to your ears, you bite the inside of your lip. Mom's words come to you in a flash. When was that? Mom asked you what the smallest country in the world was. She asked you to get her a rosary made of rosewood if you ever went to that country. The smallest country in the world. You suddenly pay attention. This country? This Vatican City?

With your earphones still on, you wander away from your group seated at the foot of the marble stairs, away from the sun, and go inside the museum alone. A rosary made of rosewood. You walk by the majestic ceiling art and a row of sculptures whose end you can't see. There has to be a gift shop somewhere, which might have a rosewood rosary for sale. As you weave quickly between people in your quest to find this rosewood rosary, you pause at the entrance to the Sistine Chapel. Michelangelo hung from the beams of that high ceiling every day for four years to work on the fresco? The sheer size of the fresco overwhelms you, so different from the way it looks in books. Yes, it would have been strange if he didn't experience physical problems after finishing this project. The artist's pain and passion gush down like water onto your face as you stand under the *Creation of Adam*. Your instincts are right; when you leave the Sistine Chapel, you immediately see a gift shop and bookstore. Nuns in white are standing behind display cases. Your eyes meet those of one particular nun.

"Are you Korean?" Korean comes out of the Sister's mouth.

"Yes."

"I came from Korea, too. You're the first Korean I've met since I was sent here. I arrived four days ago." The Sister smiles.

"Do you have rose rosaries?"

"Rose rosaries?"

"Rosaries made of rosewood?"

"Ah." The Sister takes you to one part of the display case. "Do you mean this?"

You open the rosary case the Sister hands you. The scent of roses bursts out of the airtight rosary case. Did Mom know this smell?

"It was blessed by a priest this morning."

Is this the rosewood rosary Mom talked about?

"Is this the only place you can get this rosary?"

"No, you can get it anywhere. But since it's the Vatican, there is more meaning to it if it comes from here."

You gaze at the sticker on the rosary case: fifteen euros. Your hands shake as they give the money to the nun. Still holding the rosary case, the nun asks if it's a gift. *Gift? Could I give this to Mom? Could I?* When you nod, the nun takes from the inside of the display case a white envelope with the image of the *Pietà* printed on it, puts the case inside, and seals it with a sticker.

Holding the rosewood rosary in your hand, you start walking toward St. Peter's Basilica. From the entrance, you look inside. Light cascades from the dome above the majestic bronze ciborium. Angels float among the white clouds in the ceiling fresco. You set one foot in the basilica and look beyond the large, lacquered halo. As you walk down the center aisle toward it, your feet pause. Something pulls at you, intensely. What is it? You wade through the crowd, toward the thing that is pulling at you like a magnet. You look up to see what people are looking at. The *Pietà*. The Holy Mother holding her dead son is ensconced behind bulletproof glass. As if you are being dragged forward, you push through the crowd to the front. As soon as you see the graceful image of the Holy Mother holding the body of her son, who had just breathed his last breath, you feel as though you are frozen in that spot. Is that marble? It seems that her dead son still has some heat in his body. The Holy Mother's eyes are filled with pain, as her head tilts down at her son's body laid across her lap. Even though death has already touched them, their bodies seem real—as if a poking finger would dent their flesh. The woman who was denied her motherhood still gave her lap to her son's body. They are vivid, as if alive. You feel someone brushing against your back, so you look swiftly behind you. It's as if Mom is standing behind you.

You realize that you habitually thought of Mom when something in your life was not going well, because when you thought of her it was as though something got back on track, and you felt re-energized. You still had the habit of calling Mom on the phone even after she went missing. So many days, you were about to call Mom but then stood there, numbly. You place the rosewood rosary in front of the *Pietà* and kneel. It's as if the Holy Mother's hand, cradling her dead son under his armpit, is moving. It's hard for you to look at the Holy Mother's anguish as she holds her son, who has reached death after enduring pain. You don't hear anything, and the light from the ceiling has disappeared. The cathedral of the smallest country in the world falls into deep silence. The cut in the tender skin on the inside of your lip keeps bleeding. You swallow the blood that pools in your mouth and manage to raise your head to look up at the Holy Mother. Your palms reach out automatically to touch the bulletproof glass. If you can, you want to close the Holy Mother's sorrowful eyes for her. You can sense Mom's scent vividly, as if you two had fallen asleep under the same blanket last night and you embraced her when you woke up this morning.

One winter, Mom wrapped her rough hands around your young, cold ones and took you to the furnace in the kitchen. "Oh my, your hands are sheets of ice!" You smelled the unique fragrance of Mom, who huddled around you before the fire, rubbing and rubbing your hands to warm them.

You feel the Holy Mother's fingers, which are wrapped around her dead son's body, stretching out and stroking your cheek. You remain on your knees in front of the Holy Mother, who barely manages to raise her son's hands, clearly marked by nail-inflicted wounds, until you can no longer hear footsteps in the basilica. At one point you open your eyes. You stare at the Holy Mother's lips, beneath her eyes, which are immersed in sorrow. Her lips are closed firmly, with a grace that nobody could disturb. Deep sighs escape your lips. The Holy Mother's dainty lips have moved beyond the sorrow in her eyes toward compassion. You look at her dead son again. The son's arms and legs are splayed peacefully across his mother's knees. She is soothing him even in death. If you'd told anyone in the family that you were going on a trip, they would have taken that to mean that you had given up on finding Mom. Since you had no way to convince them otherwise, you came to Rome without telling anyone. Did you come here to see the *Pietà*? When Yu-bin suggested that you join him in Italy, you might have unconsciously thought of this sculpture. Perhaps you wanted to pray in this place, pray that you could see for one last time the woman who lived in a small country attached to the edge of the vast Asian continent, to find her, and this is why you came here. Then again, maybe that wasn't it. Maybe you already understood that Mom didn't exist in this world anymore. Maybe you came here because you wanted to plead: Please don't forget Mom, please take pity on Mom. But now that you see the statue on the other side of the glass, sitting on a pedestal, embracing with her frail arms all of mankind's sorrow since the Creation, you can't say anything. You stare at the Holy Mother's lips intently. You close your eyes, back away, and leave that place. A line of priests passes, probably on their way to celebrate mass. You walk out to the entrance of the basilica and look down, dazed, at the piazza surrounded by long cloisters and enshrined in brilliant light. And only then do the words you couldn't say in front of the statue leak out from between your lips.

"Please, please look after Mom."